Horns & Wrinkles

HORNS & WRINKLES

Joseph Helgerson

illustrations by Nicoletta Ceccoli

houghton mifflin company boston

Thanks to my fellow sandbar campers: Maggie, Jake, Helen Kay,
Darlene, Pip, Bill, Rich, Pooch, and Lady. And thanks to
Kate O'Sullivan for help along the way.

Library of Congress Cataloging-in-Publication Data
Helgerson, Joseph.
Horns and wrinkles / by Joseph Helgerson ; illustrations by Nicoletta Ceccoli.
p. cm.
Summary: Along a magic-saturated stretch of the Mississippi River near Blue Wing, Minnesota,
twelve-year-old Claire and her bullying cousin Duke are drawn into an adventure involving Bodacious
Deepthink the Great Rock Troll, a helpful fairy, and a group of trolls searching for their fathers.
HC ISBN-13: 978-0-618-61679-4
PA ISBN-13: 978-0-618-98178-6

[1. Magic—Fiction. 2. Trolls—Fiction. 3. Bullies—Fiction. 4. Mississippi River—Fiction.]
I. Ceccoli, Nicoletta, ill. II. Title.
PZ7.H37408Hor 2006   [Fic]—dc22   2005025448

for
MAGGIE
JAKE
&
HELEN KAY

CLAIRE'S FAMILY

FRAN, LILLIE, & TESSA	sisters
ADAM & LINDA	parents
DUKE	cousin
PHYLLIS & NORM	aunt & uncle (Duke's parents)
GRANDPA B	grandfather
HUNTINGTON & NETTIE	great-great-great-grandparents
FLOYD	great-great-great-granduncle (Huntington's brother)

TROLL CLANS

EEL·TONGUE   Jim Dandy
                  Double-knot (Jim Dandy's father)
                  Two-cents (Jim Dandy's mother)

MOSSBOTTOM   Biz "Squeak"

FISHFLY   Stump
                  Duckwad

SLICE·TOE   Tar-and-feathers (Biz's great-aunt)

CROWLEG   Muck (Biz's wife)
                  Weed (Biz's wife)
                  Scale (Biz's wife)

DEEPTHINK   Bodacious

LEECHLICKER   Fancy (Jim Dandy's wife)

GARTOOTH   Wishy (Stump's wife)

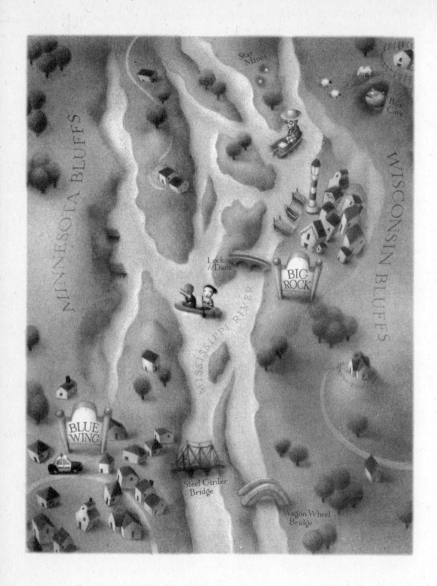

Horns & Wrinkles

FALLING

My cousin Duke's troubles on the river started the day he dangled me off the wagon wheel bridge. It's an old stone bridge, abandoned now, except for bullies and the occasional river troll in need of a hideout.

"Take it back?" Duke shouted, holding me by the ankles.

He was shaking me so hard that my lucky penny slipped out of my pocket and plopped into the river. You can take that as a sign if you want to, but it was Duke's luck, not mine, that went bad.

"Not in a million years," I told him.

The river I was hanging over was the Mississippi, which was flooding, all muddy and solid-looking as a freight train, about twenty feet below my ponytail. It was early May. None of the trees had turned green yet, but you could smell it coming fast.

I'd been out in my front yard that Saturday morning, exercising my friend Lottie, a box turtle who had wintered in my closet. Enter Duke, who'd scooped Lottie up, claiming she'd make some troll a nice snack.

Since I wasn't big enough to stop him, I pleaded with him all the way to the river, where he tossed her in. For good measure, he tried to push me in too. That was a mistake. He forgot how hard I can hold on to things — like his wrist. We landed side by side, flat on our faces in water that had been frozen ice but a short while back. Our yowls scared birds off trees.

By the time I'd struggled back to shore, floodwaters had carried Lottie away.

If I were braver, I'd have jumped in after her, but our stretch of river is a queer old chunk of water. Though nobody likes to talk about it much, the river around here is under a spell of some kind. Crippled people have been known to drive cross-country and plop down in it for a cure. And besides, I couldn't very well go after Lottie while Duke was dragging me up the bridge.

As soon as he dangled me over the edge, I saw a crutch go bobbing by beneath me, headed for New Orleans, along with all sorts of other incredible fare: a crow perched atop a dollhouse, a muskrat holding an orange tennis shoe in its mouth, a log with a dozen turtles along its spine. Maybe Lottie would hook up with them. I hoped so. With the river suffering spring fever, everything was on the move.

"You better know how to swim," Duke shouted.

It was one of his shouting days. Most were. Looking skyward, I could see up his nostrils, which seemed huge and dark as caverns.

"You know I can't," I said.

"Time you learned."

"I'll be the judge of that," I informed him, knowing better than to sound the least bit fluttery, even though I was a goner if he let go. You don't want to sound afraid of a bully, especially if he's a relative.

Duke was tall for an eleven-year-old — at least a head taller than I was even though I was a year older — and sort of pillowy soft. (Don't ever mention the pillows to him, though.) He was a fiery red-head and wore his hair short as fur, which is what it felt like if you sneaked a rub. Better not. Freckles? Lots. They were off-limits too. He was proud of his temper like peacocks are of their tails. His snub nose twitched every few seconds in case anything was cooking nearby, for if there was, he planned on being there first. He wore a black jacket with lots of zipper pockets that were full of treats and stuff confiscated from small fry.

At the moment we were disagreeing about my baseball cap, which he'd snatched while dragging me up the bridge. He was wearing it but claiming he wasn't. I can't even think why he'd want to wear a cap with a girl's name on it, except to start an argument.

"Say your prayers, Claire!" Duke shouted.

But before he could think of how to threaten me next, a sweet old voice called up to us from below.

"Excuse me," the old voice said, "have you seen a muskrat go by?"

Floating below us was a tall old lady in a red rowboat with yellow seats. She wore a blue flowery dress, a red checkered apron, and one orange tennis shoe, a high-top. Her other foot was bare. Her hands and apron had a dusting of white flour, and I caught a whiff of homemade bread.

"Beat it, you old bat!" yelled Duke.

"His name is Prince Leopold," the old lady said, unperturbed, "and he was carrying one of my sneakers."

"Can't you see I'm busy?" Duke shouted.

"I think he went that way." I pointed where the muskrat had been headed.

"You stay out of this," Duke warned me.

"Is that a girl you're holding?" the old lady politely asked. She held her hands above her eyes to shield against sun glare off the water.

"It's a warthog," Duke shouted.

"It doesn't look like a warthog." The old lady tilted her head sideways for a better view. "I'd say it looks like a girl."

"Are you calling me a liar?"

The old lady thought that over. Reaching into an apron pocket, she pulled out a pinch of what looked like flour and blew it toward us. The flour glittered in the sun and dusted my face. I'm afraid I giggled.

"Sounds like a girl," the old lady judged.

That scorched Duke's cheeks and started a rumble shimmying up his throat. The last time I'd seen him this mad was when he'd salt-and-peppered a grasshopper but couldn't make me eat it. Leaning over the edge of the bridge to aim me better, he shouted, "You asked for it!"

His grip tightened around my ankles as he positioned me for a direct hit. The old woman shook her head sadly at his efforts and called out, "You're sort of a wimp, aren't you, son?"

Squinting one eye, Duke lined me up perfectly with the rowboat and broadcast with a great deal of satisfaction, "Bombs away!"

A half-minute later nothing had happened. Between Duke's sweaty palms and my dripping socks, I began to worry that I might slip out of his grasp before he could drop me.

"I'm waiting," the old lady called out.

For ever after, Duke always claimed he might never have let go if she hadn't driven him to it.

You might think it wouldn't take long to fall twenty feet, but believe me, it can take up most of a day. My eyes were open all the way too. The wind fluttered my ponytail and tickled my one crooked tooth. I tried righting myself so that I wouldn't hit head-first, but I rolled too far and did a full somersault. Everything seemed stuck in turtle time.

Up on the bridge, Duke's eyes were large as tennis balls.

Down below, the old lady had positioned a plump cushion on the seat where I was headed. She sat with her hands folded on her lap, as if waiting for someone invited to tea. Beside the boat, a muskrat head popped out of the water, holding an orange tennis shoe in its mouth. One look at me falling out of the sky made him dive elsewhere.

Now that I was closer to the old lady, I could see that reading glasses hung around her neck on a gold chain. Wisps of white hair poofed out around a straw hat. Her face was friendly as a daisy's.

I had time to take all that in, and still I wasn't done falling. In the name of science, I decided to try an experiment and counted to ten, real slow.

After that there wasn't much doubt, but I counted to ten again, even slower, just to make sure. That made it official: something rivery was happening. At the moment, I was drifting downward with all the speed of dandelion fluff. Tucking my feet under me, I alighted on the boat cushion like a perfect lady.

"Hello," the old lady greeted. "I'm so glad you could join me."

She smiled as though we were old friends.

"Pleased to meet you," I said. "Did you do that?"

I was gesturing toward the bridge above us, the one I'd just been dropped from.

"Do what?" she asked.

A commotion from atop the bridge cut off my answer.

"My nose! My nose!"

Glancing up, I saw Duke dancing around, holding his face as if he'd just been punched on the snout. As far as I could tell, he was all alone on the bridge.

ONE HORN

Duke staggered around atop the bridge, wailing and boo-hooing as if a man-eating lion had jumped him, not that I've ever heard of lions around here. Good thing the wagon wheel bridge was so old, it had been closed to traffic, or a car would have creamed him for sure. Glancing away from my cousin, I found that the old lady had put on reading glasses and was gazing into my eyes as if I were a crystal ball.

"Do you see something?" I asked.

"River, mostly," she said, kind of distracted-like. "Some crickets."

"Is that good?" I crossed my eyes for a look myself.

"Hard to say."

The old lady gazed harder, leaning so far forward that it felt as though she might fall right inside me.

"There, there." She patted my arm kindly. "Everyone around here has a little of the river in them. And crickets aren't anything to worry about, you know. Unless they're white, of course. Then you'd have to keep an eye on them. But that boy up there, the one who mistook you for a warthog, now he's another matter. He requires a bit of worrying, I'd say. I can't put my finger on it, but there's something not quite straight about that one."

Just then Duke cut loose with a whoop ten times worse than when I'd thought a lion had him. Looking up, I saw that now *he* was being dangled over the edge of the bridge. I did a double take, thinking maybe some river trolls had nabbed him. Of course I'd never seen a river troll, only heard of them, so I couldn't be sure that I'd recognize one right away. But after a bit I could see that the pair holding Duke were only boys, about high school size. The way they were cackling, you could tell that hanging my cousin off the bridge was going to be the high point of their day.

"You big baby," one of them said, sneering.

The one talking had small mean eyes and curly blond hair that poked out like thistles. His partner had large mean eyes and straight blond hair that sat on his head like a shingle. They had split Duke's legs between them, one apiece, and were shaking him up and down while grinning like crocodiles. They'd unzipped his jacket pockets, so a steady stream of trinkets was raining on the river.

"Please, please, please," Duke blubbered.

"Whose bridge is this?" the curly blond demanded.

"Yours," Duke wailed. "Yours!"

"So who said you could use it?" the straight-haired blond asked.

"No one," Duke whimpered.

"And another thing," the curly blond went on, "we're the only ones who hang kids off this bridge."

"It won't happen again," Duke promised. "Never. I swear."

"I don't trust him," the curly blond said.

"Look at the way he's covering his face," the straight-haired blond agreed.

"Something's happened to my nose," Duke whined.

"Like what?"

"A bee sting," Duke said. "I think."

"Is he sassing us?" the straight-haired blond wanted to know.

"I'm not," Duke promised.

"Move your hands, then."

"We're not asking again either."

Duke lifted his hands away.

Even from down below I could tell that something bad had happened to my cousin's face. Something had squeezed his nose and darkened it and made it look like a coat hook.

"Ugh," grunted the curly blond, "I can't stand to hold him."

"I'd hate to meet that bee." The straight-haired blond snickered.

"Don't drop me," Duke begged. "I'll do whatever you want. Anything at all. I'll . . . I'll . . . I'll be your complete and ever-lasting toad."

"You're too ugly to be a toad."

"Way too ugly."

"But I can't swim-m-m-m-m-m."

They dropped him, then leaned over to see if he'd been lying about not being able to swim. Their pink mouths gaped like two baby crows who have just pushed a brother out of the nest.

A stone couldn't have fallen any straighter than Duke did. Headfirst all the way. There wasn't any dandelion fluff to his two-and-a-half-second fall. After splashdown, he disappeared under the old brown waters without a gurgle. At the most there were a few bubbles and a tiny whirlpool no bigger than a dinner plate. Up on the bridge, the two bullies gave each other a high five, sailed the cap Duke had been wearing — my cap — over the river, and took off. Unlike Duke, the cap landed in the rowboat, right at my feet. The old lady dusted its brim and handed it to me, saying, "Yours, I believe."

three

ONE GENUINE ACT OF KINDNESS

When Duke finally surfaced, I discovered I'd been holding my breath right along with him. We both sucked down huge lungfuls of air, though Duke gulped considerably louder. Right away he started beating the river with what seemed like six arms and legs. The brown water turned a frothy white, but he couldn't persuade it to let him stay on top.

"Better than I expected," the old lady said, impressed. "There may be some hope for him after all. Don't get me wrong. I'm not promising anything big, but he didn't give up without a fight. That usually counts for something."

Rolling up her right sleeve, the old lady leaned over the side of the rowboat and plunged her arm into the water. After a moment she hauled a waterlogged Duke out of the river by his belt, draping him over the side of the boat.

He coughed, gagged, and retched up enough river water to float a toy boat inside the rowboat. But he was alive. Mostly.

"That'll teach them," Duke coughed.

"Your cousin's a dilly," the old lady commented.

"Quiet, you," Duke threatened.

He lifted his head enough for me to see that his nose had grown a couple of inches. Its color and shape didn't look quite right either. It was darker, more pointed.

"For the record," I told Duke, "she just saved your life."

"Don't give me that," he snapped.

He snatched at my cap but his hand never got above his shoulder. Without warning, his nose shot out another inch, making him yelp and grab for it instead. From up close I could see that his nose didn't look like a coat hook at all. It looked like a horn, a baby rhinoceros horn, all gray-black and rough and curved upward.

"This is all *your* fault," he swore through his fingers.

By then the boat had drifted up against the riverbank, so Duke slogged ashore. Water ran out of his pockets. River weed clung to his cuffs. The current was so swift near shore that he had to lean forward to make any headway. When almost out of the water, he slipped on the muddy bottom, falling flat on his face. That made him bellow.

"You'll pay for this!" he cried as he crawled off through the brush. Coughing and sputtering, he added, "If it's the last thing I ever do, I'll get you. Don't think I won't. You'll . . ."

When we couldn't see him anymore and could hear him only occasionally, I asked the old lady, "Did you do that to his nose?"

"Wasn't me." She sounded envious of whoever had. "Most likely it was rock trolls. They've got a potion they sprinkle on the river around this time of the month, when the moon's almost new and the nights are blackest. All thorns and mold, the potion is. They're awfully proud of it."

Well, Duke had been in the river, so that part fit. But I'd fallen in too and didn't have anything growing on my nose, at least not that I could feel.

"Don't worry." The old lady chuckled as I patted my nose. "The potion only works on bullies."

"I've never heard of it," I said.

"You're probably not old enough, but believe me, your cousin shouldn't stick around to see if it's true. Rock trolls do collect bullies. It's a well-known fact."

"What would they want with a bully?" I asked.

"Oh, they probably line them up on shelves to admire," she said, turning kind of vague.

"Sounds like nonsense to me."

"That's because you're not a rock troll." She grew sterner. "If you were, you'd feel right at home with things like horns and hooves and what have you."

"But Duke can't go home with that thing on his face," I pointed out. "His parents will have a fit."

"That's a pity. It's certainly not safe for him around here."

"Isn't there anything he can do?" I was a little worried despite myself.

"Only one thing is tried and true. If he can manage one genuine act of kindness, the horn goes away. But it has to be a totally unselfish act. Nothing halfway."

"I don't think he's got it in him. Isn't there something easier?"

"Sorry." The old lady tsked, shaking her head no. "It's that or nothing."

A ripple beside the boat signaled that the muskrat had rejoined us. The orange tennis shoe was still in its mouth.

"So *there* you are," the old lady scolded.

Reaching down, she took the tennis shoe and pulled a folded paper from inside it. She unfolded the paper and read it with a frown.

"I'm afraid I'll have to be going." She tucked the paper into an apron pocket.

"So soon?"

"It's a big river," she said. "Awfully big. But you should be okay now."

"It's not me I'm worried about."

"Your cousin? Well, just remember this: if he gives you any trouble, a good stomp on the toe usually works wonders with a bully. Aim for the big one."

"That's not exactly what I was worrying about."

"Oh, well, fixing that nose is up to him."

She shooed me away with a wave of her hand, and I stepped off the front of the boat without even getting my shoes wet. When I turned to ask how she knew Duke was my cousin, her rowboat was gliding across the side channel that the wagon wheel bridge spanned. She wasn't using oars or a motor or anything I could see to make the boat move. She was going against the current too.

"Thank you," I called out.

"Too early for that," she answered with a wave.

"If you see a turtle named Lottie, would you please send her home?"

"I'll keep an eye out," she promised.

—four—
SUPPLIES

I pushed through twenty feet of willow saplings before Duke jumped me, though for once he didn't lay a finger on me. This time he went with words.

"It's all your fault!" he thundered.

His face was pressed as close to mine as he could get without poking me with his horn. His eyes were steady, the way they got when he'd made up his mind to take something that didn't belong to him.

"Maybe we should just head home," I suggested, holding my ground, "before something else happens."

"Are you crazy?" he half shouted. "I can't go home like this! They'll ground me for years."

He might have been exaggerating, though not by miles. Lately, his parents were strict as ants. They'd tried everything else with him, until as a last resort they'd turned to discipline.

"It's not that bad," I said, hoping to calm him.

Lowering his voice, Duke whispered, "What does it look like?"

"Well," I stalled, "a nose. A big nose."

"That's gray?" he exploded. "And pointed?"

"I've seen worse."

"Where?"

"I forget," I said. "So what do you want me to do?"

"Bring me a few supplies."

"Like what?"

"Tent, sleeping bag, slingshot, canteen, bug spray, food, matches, rain poncho, ax, fishing pole, knife, extra food, sweets, and loan me a few bucks."

He'd been doing some thinking while I'd said goodbye to the old lady.

"How many bucks?" I asked.

"Five."

As usual, he had a pretty good feel for the weight of my piggy bank.

"Where am I supposed to get all that other stuff?"

"My garage. Use your little sister's wagon to get it out here."

With that, he hung his head helplessly. It was mostly an act, but he had a gift for it.

"Look," I said, "the old lady told me how you can fix your nose."

"How?" Right away he turned suspicious.

"All you have to do is one genuine act of kindness and it's gone."

That news straightened him up in a flash. I couldn't have done it any faster by stomping on his big toe, which, in a way, I had. If pride had toes, I'd nailed Duke's. He bragged about bad deeds, not kind ones.

"Don't be so dumb," Duke nagged. "That old bat doesn't know anything."

"Have it your way," I sighed.

"So you'll get the supplies?"

"I guess. This once."

The instant I agreed to help, his face lit up with such rare thankfulness and gratitude that I nearly staggered backwards. The makeover didn't last long, though.

"Don't mess up," he threatened.

He started to reach for my cap, having forgotten all about his new nose and how it shot out farther every time he bullied. To protect him from himself, I stomped on his right big toe — his flesh-and-blood one — and left him hopping around on one foot.

"I'll be back as soon as I can," I said.

"And bring a mirror," Duke ordered, losing his balance and falling sideways into some bushes.

—five—
AUNT PHYLLIS

The old lady had set us off on the big island across from Blue Wing, the town where we lived. To get home all I had to do was find the sandy lane leading to the steel girder bridge that spanned the river's main channel and connected the island to town.

From up on the big bridge, you can get a pretty good view of Blue Wing, which is built on a flat old sandbar that sits in the shadows of the bluffs crowding the river. It's the kind of place that shines up good in the moonlight, with lots of crooked old buildings built over a forgotten Indian village. The only hill in town is a dike built to keep out the floods.

I hustled home to get my sister Tessa's red wagon, plus a few cookies from the kitchen, a couple of apples for vitamins, some cans of tomato soup that nobody liked, and a bag of pretzels for starch. I shook my piggy bank dry, then put a dollar back. Where was Duke going to spend money on a sandbar?

From my place to Duke's was only a couple of blocks. He lived in a tidy white house with potted petunias out front and a picket fence that kept their springer spaniel, Duff, from wandering off. Duke's dad, Norm, ran the No Leash Dog Obedience College, and Duff never barked unless ordered to. That was good—I didn't want a dog sounding the alarm while I loaded up on supplies. All I had to do was make sure Duke's parents weren't home, which was a cinch. Both their cars were gone.

Since the neighbors knew me, I went directly to the garage without pretending to knock on any doors. I was climbing up a stepladder to reach a sleeping bag tucked in the rafters when the door opened and in stepped Duke's mom. She didn't bother asking why I was filling a red wagon with stuff from her garage.

"What's he done now?" she whispered with a trembly voice.

Duke's mom, Phyllis, was a school nurse who spent her days handing out hugs and Band-Aids. She was small, what my mom called petite, and liked to wear jeans and T-shirts with pictures of things like the three basic food groups on them. Duke's dad, Norm, was an even softer touch. They were the kind of parents you long for when your own are acting up. Where they'd gone wrong with Duke weighed on them night and day, stooping their shoulders, stealing their sleep, and making them decide that one child was their limit.

"He's thinking about doing some camping," I reported, "and needed a few things."

Unless you were Duke, Aunt Phyllis wasn't someone you ever thought about lying to.

"Why'd he send you?"

"Well" — I hesitated — "he's sort of busy getting his campsite ready."

"What else?" Aunt Phyllis asked bravely.

"I guess there was a little accident," I admitted.

Her shoulders stiffened.

"Nothing catastrophic," I assured her. "He just didn't want to bother you, that's all."

"He'd rather have us worry all night about whether he's alive and have the police looking for him and maybe even the National Guard. Is that it?"

Her voice was rising.

"Well," I fudged, "something's, ah, happened to his nose."

"Fighting again?" Aunt Phyllis guessed, biting her lip to stop tears.

"Not that I know of."

Which was mostly true. He hadn't put up much of a fight with the two older bullies.

"Worse?" Aunt Phyllis's eyes widened.

"It's growing kind of funny."

When I held a finger three or four inches in front of my face to show her how funny, she covered her mouth with a hand and started blinking real hard. Her shock lasted only a minute, though. She was a school nurse, after all, and had seen a lot. Turning professional, she grabbed my arm, saying, "Take me to him."

And that's how I ended up in the back of Aunt Phyllis's minivan with Duke's eyes shooting lightning and hailstones at me as we drove straight to the hospital.

DR. E. O. MONEYBAKER & ONE·SHOT

Doctors came, doctors went. Some swooped in for a nose-to-nose examination. Others stayed put in the hallway, holding a tissue over their own noses as if Duke might be contagious. They poked at Duke, shined bright lights on him. Shaking their heads, they went to get other doctors. The parade lasted through the rest of the morning and on into the afternoon.

X-rays, needles, questions — the works.

Where had he been? What had he been doing? Why had he waited so long to come in?

Duke answered everything with his terribly innocent voice, the one that makes teachers bite their tongues and go red in the face.

The only doctor who believed a word of what Duke had to say was the very last one, who arrived after supper and billed himself as the local rhinoceros horn expert. They'd had to call him in from the old folks' home, which explained why Dr. E. O. Moneybaker used two canes, two hearing aids, and two pairs of eyeglasses. Actually, he wore only one set of eyeglasses, but they were as thick as two.

The doctor wasn't traveling alone either. At his side slouched a short grumpy man with a black mustache that bristled like porcupine quills. A large camera hung around the sidekick's neck. He snapped pictures for the local newspaper and everyone called him One-shot, on account of that's all he needed to get the job done. He wore a rumpled black suit with pockets that sagged with film canisters and sandwiches and things.

"My picture going to be in the paper?" Duke asked, perking up.

"Not a chance," One-shot told him.

"He's here at my request," Dr. E. O. Moneybaker said in a weak, raspy voice. "I've been writing a scientific paper on these horns for years. If I'm ever going to see it in the *New England Journal of Medicine*, I'll need photographs."

"You've seen this condition before?" Aunt Phyllis was hovering.

"Most definitely," the doctor replied, pulling out a cloth tape measure and holding it up to Duke's horn. After scribbling measurements down in a notebook, he waved One-shot forward, saying, "Front and side view, please."

"Front, side, top, bottom," One-shot said, swinging into action, "it doesn't matter, Doc, and you know it." To Aunt Phyllis, he explained, "I've been taking pictures along this stretch of river for going on thirty years, seen stuff that turned my hair white, but none of it ever shows up on film."

"There's not a white hair on your head," the doctor objected.

"'Course not. I have to dye it about once a week, the stuff I've seen along this river."

Snapping a shot of Duke's front and side, One-shot promised he'd run the film over to Dr. Moneybaker's residence before gnat time was over. (Around here, that's dusk.) The doctor waved the photographer on his way and turned his attention to Duke's ears, peering inside them with a light.

"Is he going to be all right?" Aunt Phyllis asked.

"Hard to say," Dr. Moneybaker said. "Sometimes this condition clears up all on its own, almost overnight. Sometimes it gets worse.

Hooves have been known to develop." Pulling out a magnifying glass, he picked up one of Duke's hands for a look. "Nothing there yet."

"Is that all?" Aunt Phyllis braced herself for the worst.

"In about half of the cases I've seen," the doctor rambled on, checking down the back of Duke's pants, "patients have been known to disappear." Letting go of Duke's pants, he added, "No tail yet. We're not exactly sure what makes them disappear. Maybe they run away. Maybe they're taken. Sometimes there's a sign of struggle. All that we can say for positive is that once they're gone, they don't come back."

"Heavens!" Aunt Phyllis gasped. "How can I not have heard of this? I'm a school nurse."

"Oh, well, I see a case only once or twice a year at the most. And you know how hush-hush families get when they think something rivery is going on. The main thing is not to let him out of your sight." Reaching into a pocket, the doctor pulled out a purple dog leash. "This should help with that."

"Whoa," Duke squawked. "I'm not wearing anything that's purple."

"Don't worry," the doctor told Aunt Phyllis, "they all talk tough at first."

"Listen, you old wreck . . ." Duke started to say, but before he could finish his insult, he cried out and made a grab for his nose, which was having a growth spurt again.

"Isn't there anything else we can do?" Aunt Phyllis pleaded.

"Nothing that's been proven," the doctor stated, holding up his magnifying glass to Duke's nose.

"What about a genuine act of kindness?" I asked, feeling silly but figuring I'd better mention it. Aunt Phyllis was looking as though the world might end any second.

I expected to be shushed by Aunt Phyllis, or shoulder-punched by Duke, but before either could act, the doctor took an interest in my question, saying, "Have you had contact with an old lady in a rowboat?"

"That old biddy," Duke muttered.

"She was involved in my very first case of rhinohornitis," the doctor told him. "Fifty some years back she showed up in a rowboat— was an old woman back then too. She's figured in about half the cases I've seen."

"Enough!" Duke wailed. "That old goat didn't have anything to do with my nose. Just give me a pill or something and let's get out of this dump."

"Has he always carried on like this?" the doctor asked.

"Pretty much," Aunt Phyllis admitted, embarrassed.

"Well, *that* is something I can give you a pill for. We've found it to be quite effective in cases like this."

About dusk, we left the hospital with some pretty pink pills. Duke's nose was bandaged up neat as a package, and there was a dog leash attached to his wrist.

THE FIRST HORN IN OUR FAMILY

Fast as news travels around Blue Wing, you'd think everyone ran a newspaper. By the time I got home, Mom and Dad and my three sisters were camped out on the front porch, waiting. Mom was still dressed for the department store, where she works, and hadn't started supper yet. Dad, who works the graveyard shift at the bakery, must have just woken up, 'cause he was still in his pajamas. My youngest sister, Tessa, clung to her Barbie doll. Lillie of a thousand moods, my older sister, sat closest to the inside door, in case the phone rang. My other older sister, Fragile Fran, had her headphones on, as always. Even Grandpa Bridgewater had come over for the show. He was the first to pipe up.

"Hear tell we've got another horn in the family."

"What do you mean, another one?" I asked.

"First things first, young lady," warned my mother, who wasn't about to let Grandpa B sidetrack her. "Just what have you and Duke been up to now?"

So I told them, and since they all knew Duke, they were mostly satisfied that I couldn't have done much differently, except maybe not worry so much about Lottie. Parts of what I told them lifted some eyebrows, though none that belonged to my sisters. They were too busy acting bored to lift anything but a sigh. That's a stage they're stuck in, except when I bring home some poor starving frog or beetle or garter snake. The way my sisters dance then, you'd think the house was on fire. They're dead set against boarders and always accuse me of trying to be the son that Dad never had. I don't know about that, but I do know that reptiles and amphibians seem to understand me way better than my sisters do.

Anyway, as soon as I'd finished, everyone's eyes shifted to Grandpa, wanting to hear about the other horn in our family.

"This going to be an Uncle Floyd story?" my dad asked, which meant that he'd probably heard it before but never mentioned it because of my mom, who doesn't approve of river stories.

"Thereabouts," Grandpa admitted. "Might have a rock troll or two in it."

Then nothing got said for a bit as Grandpa got his facts straight. He was a knobby old guy in his eighties, prone to coughing fits, felt hats, and getting lost. While waiting, I couldn't spy a neighborhood kid moving, or feel a breeze shuffling, or hear a clock ticking. The whole world seemed to be hanging on what he had to say.

"So?" Mom prodded at last. "Uncle Floyd?"

"Yup," Grandpa B said. "The one who was the younger brother of you girls' Great-Great-Great-Grandpa Huntington. Actually, Huntington had a horn for a bit too."

Everyone exchanged looks, the way we always did during Grandpa B's stories.

"Was that before or after his lumber mill went bust?" Dad calmly asked.

"Oh, before. Right after him and Floyd got run out of Missouri for their bullying."

"Bullying?" I said.

"You didn't think Duke was the only one of those in the family, did you?"

"And the horns?" Dad prompted.

"Those happened the first winter they were up here. They'd chopped a hole in the river ice to scrub up some and the next thing they knew . . ."

"Horns," I said, filling in the blank.

"Yup. They both had 'em, and they were growing every now and then too."

"When they bullied someone," I guessed.

"Chances are," Grandpa B agreed. "And then one day in late March, or maybe it was early April, just about the time when the ice was going out, they heard a real ruckus down to the river. Huntington dashed down there and found a pretty young lady trapped on an ice floe with a flock of sheep. They were floating away from shore, farther and farther every second, with no hope of ever getting ashore, not unless someone came to their rescue."

"Couldn't she swim?" Lillie asked, astonished.

"Not a stroke. And particularly not in the river. Back then folks thought the river just sucked you right under. Today it's lots calmer."

"Did they go to her rescue?" I asked.

"Certainly did. Huntington nearly drowned himself doing it. He could hardly swim a lick himself, but somehow or other, he got that young lady and all her flock ashore. Cold as that water was, he was blue as a jay by the time he was done. But when he climbed out of the river, he'd shed his horn and had his own handsome Bridgewater nose back."

"He'd done an act of genuine kindness," I whispered to myself.

No one was paying much attention to me, though. They were waiting for Grandpa to finish the story. He knew it too. You could tell by the way his shoelaces all of a sudden needed retying, and then his pocket watch needed winding, and then he got to working on his neck, where he always got a kink whenever you tried to hurry him along.

"All right," Mom complained, tapping a foot, "what about this Uncle Floyd? What happened to him? You said it was his story too."

"Oh, he stayed on shore, calling Huntington coarse names," Grandpa B said.

"So he didn't lose his horn?"

"Not that day. I think it even grew a little. There was a lamb or two that went missing around suppertime."

"Did he ever lose his horn?" Fran asked.

"Don't know," Grandpa confessed, putting a hand over his heart to show that he was telling us exactly what he'd been told himself, without any of his famous add-ons. "He disappeared about a week later, never to be seen again. He went down to the river one night, to fetch a bucket of water, and never came back."

"Are you sure about that?" Dad asked.

"Heard that part on good faith from the young lady that Huntington saved."

"How'd you ever get a chance to ask her such a question?" Mom was eyeing Grandpa suspiciously.

"Well, she turned out to be my Great-Grandmother Nettie— great-great-great to you girls—who lived to a very ripe old age and had a talk with me when I was a sprout."

"What was she like?" Lillie wanted to know.

"Pretty as you, and kindly."

"So what happened to Floyd?" I said.

"Rock trolls," Grandpa B reported with a satisfied nod.

"Don't you think," Mom asked, "that it's far more likely that he somehow fell into the river and drowned?"

"Along this stretch of river?" Grandpa scoffed. "Why, who knows what might have happened, but I can tell you this much for sure: old Huntington never saw his brother again, even though he more than once offered to give away everything he owned if it would bring Floyd back. I think he felt kind of to blame, him being the eldest and all."

Grandpa looked about to launch into further details, but a station wagon whipped up in front of our house without cutting its headlights. A sour-looking Dr. E. O. Moneybaker struggled out the passenger door. One-shot, who'd been driving, tried to lend the doctor a hand but got waved off.

Once I explained who they were, everyone stampeded down to meet them.

"Bad pictures," Dr. Moneybaker barked, waving a grainy print under the streetlight beside our sidewalk. "We're trying to find Duke so we can take another batch."

"Isn't he home?" my mother asked.

"Not at the moment," the doctor groused, dabbing at his forehead with a folded hanky, "though his folks are. I'm afraid there's been a small accident."

"How small?" Grandpa called out. Aunt Phyllis was his youngest child.

"It appears," the doctor said, blinking at us through his thick eyeglasses, "that Duke's parents have been turned to stone."

There was a general all-round gasp.

"Stone?" Grandpa B fumed, pushing his way up front. "What kind of stone?"

"Does it matter?"

"And you call yourself a doctor?" Grandpa B snapped. "Gangway! There might still be time to save 'em."

eight

STONE

Grandpa always shed about seventy years whenever anything rivery was going on, so he got to Duke's front door first. Without knocking he barged in, declaring, "It's me."

Right behind Grandpa came Dad, still in his pajamas, who called out, "Phyllis?"

The rest of us crowded in behind Grandpa and Dad, none too brave. So far as I knew, no one in our family had ever been turned to stone before.

When Dr. E. O. Moneybaker and One-shot arrived, the doctor announced, "They're in the kitchen."

Everyone flocked to the back of the house, straining not to touch anything on the way. The rooms were so still and watchful that there had to be a spell at work somewhere. In the living room, the old-fashioned mantel clock was still ticking, but its hands kept bouncing off 8:28, as if some hidden wall were keeping them from reaching the next minute.

We all squeezed into the kitchen, where the empty purple leash was lying on the floor and the back door was hanging wide open. There was no sign of Duke. His parents were facing each other across the breakfast nook, still as the bowl of plastic fruit between them. They were stone statues, all right, yellowish sandstone of the kind that shows up here and there along the river. Kids loved to scratch their names and the year into the stuff.

Uncle Norm had been zapped while patting Aunt Phyllis's hand. He was a large kindly man who had never met a dog who didn't want to lick him. At the moment, he was sitting with his mouth hanging opening, looking as though he were saying famous last words.

Aunt Phyllis's head was tilted slightly forward, as if petrified in the middle of a woeful nod yes. Crouching at their feet, just as solid as they were, was Duff, the family spaniel. That explained why we hadn't been bowled over and licked clean as a spoon when we stepped through the front door.

Then I noticed something about Aunt Phyllis.

"What's that?" I said, pointing.

One of Aunt Phyllis's cheeks was moist. As we watched, a tear gathered at the corner of her stone eye and seeped downward.

"We're not too late," Grandpa called out, twice as loud as necessary. "But we'll need some river water to save 'em."

"How much river water?" Dad asked.

"Fill this," Grandpa said, grabbing Uncle Norm's silver thermos off the kitchen counter. "And quick. Don't spare the horses."

nine

MORE STONE

Duke lived just seven blocks from the river, but it seemed to be taking Dad most of forever to get back. Finally, Tessa couldn't take it any longer.

"Grandpa, what happened to Aunty and Unc?" she asked.

"River trolls."

"You don't know that," Mom protested.

"Sure do," Grandpa replied. "Your second cousin Alfie had a run-in with some of 'em down to Five Creeks. They turned him into stone just like this."

"River trolls?" Dr. E. O. Moneybaker snorted. "This is the first I've heard of them being involved. All the old wives' tales blame this kind of nonsense on rock trolls."

Grandpa scoffed, saying, "Haven't you ever heard the saying 'River trolls use rocks and rock trolls use river'?"

"Well, of course I have," the doctor crabbed, "but as a man of science, I'm not convinced it means anything."

"And I suppose you think these two people here haven't been turned to stone either," Grandpa said, resting his case.

The doctor worked his jaw up and down plenty without thinking of a comeback to that. Finally, he turned away from Grandpa and snapped at One-shot, "More pictures."

"They won't turn out any better than the ones of the kid," One-shot predicted, but he started clicking close-ups and side shots. Meanwhile, Dr. Moneybaker was tugging on a pair of surgical gloves lifted from a pocket, sliding his eyeglasses on top of his head, and leaning over Aunt Phyllis.

"Those gloves won't protect you any," Grandpa warned. "Not with stone this fresh. It's got to sit for years before it's safe to touch stone such as this."

"Don't interrupt," the doctor grumbled.

"Gloves didn't help Cousin Ernie," Grandpa said.

"Who's Cousin Ernie?" I asked.

"Cousin Alfie's brother."

"Cousin Alfie being the one turned to stone down to Five Creeks?" asked Dr. Moneybaker, who'd stopped leaning toward the breakfast nook.

"Yup," Grandpa nodded. "And Cousin Ernie couldn't stop himself from touching Alfie, just to make sure he'd really been turned to stone. 'Course, he got turned to stone too, the instant he touched Alfie. And even though he had sense enough to put on a pair of leather gloves before he went touching anything."

"And how, pray tell," the doctor said, "did they turn him to stone?"

"Wouldn't know," Grandpa cheerfully admitted. "Do I look like some kind of river troll to you?"

"Dad," my mom spliced in, using her be-nice tone, "who told you this story?"

"Got it straight from the horse's mouth," Grandpa said. "Alfie and Ernie told it to me, and anyone else who cared to listen. Not many did."

"So they didn't stay stone?" I asked.

"At least somebody's listening," Grandpa declared, pleased. "Ernie no more than touched Alfie and got sha-zammed to stone, than someone came up behind them and pushed them both into the river. Soon as they hit the water they got turned back to flesh and bone. My personal opinion? The river water saved them."

"How long ago did all this happen?" the doctor asked, fumbling for his notebook.

"Oh, they were young fellows then," Grandpa allowed. "Didn't know any better. It would have been back in the Depression."

The fact that it had happened seventy some years ago didn't bother the doctor in the slightest. Right away he asked Grandpa if he'd ever heard of anyone growing a horn like Duke's.

"Of course I have," Grandpa said, dragging out the story of Huntington Bridgewater and his brother Floyd.

Having to tell a story twice never slowed Grandpa down any. What's more, the doctor scribbled notes and even asked Grandpa to repeat dates and places. Grandpa was pretty near in heaven.

They were still at it when the siren came woo-wooing down the street, cutting off right in front of the house. Seconds later came a *bam-bam-bam* at the front door. Rushing through the living room, we found Dad still in his pajamas and looking kind of sheepish. Standing next to him was a tall, thin sheriff's deputy who was holding Uncle Norm's thermos.

ten

EVEN MORE STONE

Y̶ou got a couple of people turned to stone in there?" the deputy
asked.

"We certainly do," Mom answered.

"Then you better let this man through," the deputy said, handing
Dad the thermos. "He's carrying river water."

"Home remedies won't help," Dr. Moneybaker scoffed.

"You some kind of doc?" the deputy said, sizing him up.

"I am."

"You ever heard of fish scales?" the deputy asked.

"Don't be impertinent."

"On people?" the deputy persisted.

"Of course on people. Around here I've heard of everything."

"Good," the deputy said. "Then maybe you can tell us what's the
best way to get rid of fish scales."

"As a general rule, you don't."

"Tell that to my Aunt Buffy," the deputy shot back.

"Let me guess," Grandpa B said. "River water?"

"Mixed with a little mustard and goose fat," the deputy agreed
with a nod. "So when I pull a guy over for speeding, and he's wearing pajamas and holding a thermos between his legs, the first thing I

do is ask what's in the thermos. When he says, 'River water,' I say, 'Better let me see.' And when it really turns out to be river water, I help him get to wherever he's going—fast. We've got orders directly from the sheriff himself on that one. So step aside in the name of the law."

"Now, hold on here," Dr. Moneybaker balked. "I haven't conducted any tests yet."

But he said it from behind us. Dad had already pushed past him, and the rest of us weren't collecting dust either.

"Where you planning on pouring it?" the deputy asked.

That question brought Dad to a dead stop in the living room, right in front of the stalled mantel clock.

"Does it matter?" Dad said.

"It can make all the difference in the world," the deputy told him. "Aunt Buffy got her best results by pouring it over her heart, even though the scales were on the back of her legs."

"Uh-uh," One-shot disagreed. "I've always heard you should pour on the top of the head."

"From what I've heard," Mom said, "you pour where the spell touched them first."

Hearing that from Mom stunned us all. She never admitted to having the least bit of interest in river gossip.

"How do we know where they got touched first?" Dad wondered.

"Time's a-wasting," Grandpa blurted, and, grabbing the thermos from Dad, he took off for the kitchen, where he skidded to a stop in front of the breakfast nook.

Grandpa was unscrewing the thermos cap when Dr. Moneybaker shoved his way forward, saying, "I still need a sample of the moisture on that woman's cheek." He lunged for the thermos.

Grandpa B and the doctor were both old as the hills, but Grandpa's hills were in better shape, and he was winning until the deputy tried to separate them. They all got tangled up with each other and toppled forward, falling into the breakfast nook.

I closed my eyes, afraid to watch. When I opened them, there were five stone statues crammed in that breakfast nook. Six if you counted Duff. Dr. Moneybaker was sprawled across Uncle Norm's back. The deputy was standing on one leg, with a hand on Aunt Phyllis's arm for balance. Grandpa was stretched out beneath the table, the back of his head touching Duff's tail. His mouth was open as if about to shout something colorful.

The thermos with the river water had gone flying, so I retrieved it and with some help from Dad unscrewed the cap. Pouring river water over their heads didn't undo anything, though. They looked as stony as ever, and wet. Aunt Phyllis kept right on tearing up too. Those of us who hadn't been turned to stone weren't too surprised—Grandpa's stories weren't known for their accuracy.

eleven

CATFISH, BUFFALO, POTS OF GOLD

The clocks may have been stuck, but the phone, though full of static, was still working. Dad didn't waste any time getting ahold of the police. Hearing that a deputy had been lost to stone, the dispatcher immediately rang the sheriff at home.

Sheriff Tommy Pope wore a crisp brown uniform with a shiny bronze star directly over his heart. The top button of his shirt was undone, but nothing else about him said he'd been relaxing at home. His well-padded gut and gray sideburns made him look as capable and dependable in person as he did in all his re-election posters, the same posters that sprouted up all over town every four years as if by magic.

What the sheriff's reelection posters didn't prepare you for was a talker. One glance at the breakfast nook had him sighing as if he'd been through all this a hundred-plus times before. Without introducing himself, he leaned back against the kitchen counter, hitched his thumbs inside his belt, and said, "First things first. One-shot, it's time for you to hit the road. The last thing we need is a newspaper man hanging around."

"You know that paper of mine," One-shot protested. "It won't go anywhere near a story like this. Not for anything."

"Still and all," the sheriff said, "these people might like some privacy."

"Oh." One-shot acted a little embarrassed for not seeing that himself. "Sorry," he added, and with a nod, he left.

We scrunched together a little closer to hear what the sheriff might say next.

"There's folks in this town that choose not to believe in fortunetelling catfish, or low-flying buffalo, or whatever," the sheriff remarked, staring at a spot on the ceiling rather than at us. "I'll tell you straight out, I'm not one of them. After all I've seen during my years of sheriffing, I'll believe most anything and then some. Even these TV talk shows wouldn't touch half the things I've had reported to me. There's a woman over on Huff Street with talking mice in her walls. The thing is, I've had a word or two with them myself. Real polite, they are. And you can't hardly get by a rainbow around here without two or three honest citizens calling to ask if anyone's lost a pot of gold. And that new housing addition out west of town? There's a coyote trying to burn it down. I've seen it running around with a flaming branch in its mouth. Not to mention the troll sightings, ogre swindles, and blue-wing fairy disturbances." Lowering his gaze to us, he went on, "What I'm getting at is this — you can feel free to tell me exactly what's happened here. I won't be poking fun at it or spreading it around. On that you can be sure. Antagonizing voters isn't my style at all."

So Dad told him. The sheriff un-huhed and ahem-ed through everything. When Dad pointed to the stopped clock on the mantel, the sheriff clicked his tongue and said that spells generally raised hob with clocks. When Dad got to the part about his being escorted back by a deputy, the sheriff smiled proudly and confided, "That's what I tell 'em. If somebody's rushing somewhere with river water, help 'em get there. Time's a-wasting."

"The river water didn't help," Mom said.

"Generally doesn't," the sheriff agreed. "Always worth a try, though."

After Dad finished the rest of his story, the sheriff nodded thoughtfully and crossed over to the wide-open back door.

"Not a scratch." He whistled lowly in admiration as he shined a flashlight on the lock. "There never is. Two or three times a month we find 'em open like this. You won't be able to close this door for years." To show us what he meant, he slammed the door shut and quickly stepped away. It flew back open immediately, as if flung by an unseen hand. "Unless you're willing to leave it open until the spell wears off, the only thing you can do with a door like this is pay Secondhand Tim to haul it away. He's got a back room full of 'em."

Still admiring the door, the sheriff added, "If you folks don't mind staying put, I think I'll take a spin around the backyard and see what I can see. I don't imagine there's anything out there to worry about, but best to be on the safe side, don't you think?"

As the sheriff went down the back steps, we packed ourselves around the door, not wanting to miss anything.

First off, the sheriff squatted on his haunches to point his flashlight at Aunt Phyllis's vegetable patch, which was freshly tilled for spring planting. He must have been looking for footprints in the loose dirt, as it was too early for any vegetables to be sprouting. After that he worked his way over to the white picket fence, where it ran along the alley, and walked its length, stopping here and there to sweep his light around. Once he stood still for nearly a minute, as if he'd found something. We all leaned forward. That's when he pulled a leafy willow branch free from two pickets, except that it couldn't have been a leafy willow branch. There wasn't a tree around that had leafed out yet.

"Troll tracks," the sheriff explained, once back in the kitchen. "Three sets of them, which is the usual number they travel in." He held up the willow branch. "River trolls, not rock."

"You can tell that from a willow branch?" Dad said.

"Forget the willow branch," the sheriff corrected. "This here is a hair off a genuine river troll, or so I'm told. Never seen one myself. They're tricky brutes."

At first we all edged back, but then we changed our minds and inched closer. The branch in the sheriff's hand was thinner and more leathery than anything off a tree. It smelled different too, more fishy than foresty.

"So what are we supposed to do?" Mom asked, pinching my arm hard enough to leave welts. Her other hand was doing the same to Tessa, and if she'd had two more hands, they would have been clamped onto Lillie and Fran.

"This particular spell's solid as can be," the sheriff said. "Waiting's not really an option, unless you've got a century or two to spare. I'm told there's only one thing to be done with stone like this, and that's hunt up the trolls responsible. They're the ones who can reverse what's happened here."

"And how are we supposed to find them?" Dad wanted to know.

"That's a problem, all right," the sheriff agreed. "I'd put out an all points bulletin, but that might get picked up by a reporter, which I'm afraid would only cause more problems than it'd solve. Publicity drives the slightest little rivery thing underground. Our best success has come from working closely with the family. Believe it or not, you're the ones who know the most about what happened here today. Doesn't have to be anything big or exciting that started all this. It doesn't take much to set off a troll, and there must have been some funny business going on here. If my eyes don't deceive me, that's Dr. E. O. Moneybaker turned to stone over there. And I know for a fact that he doesn't make house calls for your run-of-the-mill aches and pains."

I checked in with Dad, who nodded for me to go ahead and tell everything.

"Well, our cousin Duke," I volunteered, "he's got a rhino horn where his nose used to be."

"There you go," the sheriff said, encouraged. "That's a start. I can tell you from experience that nothing draws trolls like a rhino horn, though from what I hear it's usually rock trolls that come calling."

From there I spilled the rest of what had happened to Duke.

"That wagon wheel bridge," the sheriff muttered, shaking his head when I'd finished. "It's a real hangout, all right. Well, here's what I suggest we do. First, we form a search party. If we haven't any luck by morning, we enlist as many kids as we can to help us. They've got the best eyes for spotting anything rivery. Either way, once we find these trolls, we offer each of them a dollar."

"We may not be rich," Mom interrupted, "but we can certainly afford more than a dollar."

"No need to," the sheriff assured her. "A dollar's a fortune to a troll, though it's got be silver, not paper. That old coin shop downtown keeps some silver ones on hand for emergencies like this."

"All right." Dad nodded. "Is there anything else we have to know?"

"Well, there is one other thing." The sheriff surveyed us all. "Common sense, really, but I mention it in case some of you haven't heard. If you do meet up with some river trolls, whatever you do, don't mention their fathers."

Nods all around to that. Everyone knew that bringing up a troll's father was about the worst possible thing you could do.

"Has anyone ever turned a spell back?" Mom asked, real quiet-like.

"I won't lie to you," the sheriff told her. "Reversals are a rare thing. But I've heard on good authority that it has been done a time or two. Now I suggest we seal off this house and get rolling while the trail's still warm."

twelve

A LATE-NIGHT VISITOR

We couldn't shut the back door with nails, cinder blocks, or duct tape. The nails popped, the blocks tumbled, the tape split — and the door flew open. In the end we hung one of Uncle Norm's Beware of Dog signs on the door handle to keep gawkers away.

"Have to do," the sheriff said. "I want to get you over to the wagon wheel bridge before midnight."

The "you" the sheriff was referring to was me. I was to show him right where everything happened. On the way there, the sheriff swung by the coin shop he had mentioned, which had a light on despite the hour. The shop had a green door with frosty glass on the upper half and painted gold letters that read:

> COINS, GEMS, RUNESTONES,
> RIDDLES & OTHER IMPONDERABLES
> WING REPAIR ON OCCASION

The sheriff was in and out in barely a minute, handing over three silver dollars to my dad, who'd come along for the ride.

"Hang on to these," the sheriff ordered. "There's one for each troll, but don't go handing them over until they've done what you're paying them for."

Dad nodded that he understood. From there, it was on to the wagon wheel bridge.

According to the dash clock, we got to the bridge by eleven. There weren't any old ladies in rowboats to be seen, though we did spot a Day-Glo orange sneaker go floating by. I snagged it with a branch. Without bothering to ask what I was up to, the sheriff handed me a pocket-size notebook along with a pen, then shined his flashlight over my shoulder so that I could see what I was writing. I printed out a note that politely asked for help in finding Duke. Tearing out the sheet, I stuffed it into the shoe and tossed it back into the river. Nothing happened, though. The old lady never showed up.

We did hear some strange echoes—popping bubbles, squishy footsteps—from under the bridge. A Duke-ish kind of snicker found us, but when I said his name, no answer.

"Louder," the sheriff whispered.

"Duke," I sang out, "your mom and dad have been turned to stone. Grandpa B too."

A splash.

"And that doctor who tried to help you?" I called out. "He got it too."

Ripples.

"And one of my deputies," the sheriff added. "Which brings in the law."

A glugging, laughing sound, which drew the sheriff's flashlight beam, but we didn't see a thing. He turned the light off, waited a few seconds, and snapped it back on, hoping to surprise someone, but he didn't. We kept it up for close to a half hour without any luck.

"Tomorrow's going to be a long one," the sheriff said as he drove us home. "Better get some rest."

Mom said the same thing as she tucked me into bed. Of course, everyone was too wound up to fall asleep right away, and I could hear my sisters tossing and turning past midnight. Dad had Saturday night off from the bakery, but he didn't plan on getting any rest at all before beginning the search. He changed out of his PJs, grabbed a flashlight, and dashed back to the river just as a storm started edging toward town. Distant thunder rattled the windows, and you could smell rain coming, lots of it.

A sleepless hour passed before I heard the sound at my window. At first I thought the *scritch-scritch-scritch* was the wind making a branch scratch the glass, or at least that's what I was hoping. But the pitiful *me-eow* that followed wouldn't have fooled a toy cat. When I pulled up my window shade, there he was, sitting in the catalpa tree right next the house—Duke.

thirteen

DUKE'S FAVOR

My cousin's horn was two or three times bigger than before, and more rhinocerosy than ever. The rest of him looked the same, though, if you skipped over a black eye and mud-caked clothes.

"Where have you been?" I whispered through the screen.

"Hanging around with some cool guys."

"They got names?"

"Yup. One apiece."

"So what do you want?" I took a deep breath. Duke can drive you crazy when he thinks he knows something you don't.

"A favor," Duke said. "This whole business is your fault, you know."

"In your mind." I laughed. "Besides, what could you possibly need help with?"

"Mining."

"That's not exactly my specialty," I pointed out, but he had me hooked.

He knew it too. The only mining around here isn't done by people, and it isn't open to the public. Sometimes late at night you can sort of hear, maybe feel, a thud from deep in the earth. Rock trolls, everyone says. Up to their tricks, although nobody knows what those tricks might be. Here and there you might meet some-one who claimed to have caught a glimpse of a river troll. But rock trolls? Nobody. What exactly Duke was up to, I had no idea, but I could see teeth beneath his horn, which probably meant he was grinning.

"You'll get on-the-job training," he pledged.

"That one of your famous promises?"

"You bet."

All right, so maybe I should have been calling out to Mom instead of trading smart talk, but the thing is, even though Duke looks pil-lowy, he can be fast as a weasel when he needs to be. If I'd sounded the alarm, he'd have dropped off the branch and vanished in a snap. So I played along, hoping to buy some time and maybe find a way to help Grandpa B, Aunt Phyllis, Uncle Norm, and the others—including Duke. If you asked why it mattered if Duke ever came home at all, I guess I'd have to say because every kid deserves a home—even him.

"What do you want me to do?" I asked.

"Help us buy some mining supplies." I was about to tell him I was broke, but he boasted, "We've got the money."

"So why do you need me?"

"None of us can come into town. At least not when any stores are open."

"I can see why you can't," I stated. "What about your friends?"

"They don't go into towns."

I couldn't squeeze anything more out of him, and the drop or two I'd gotten sounded like more lie than truth. But it was enough. One of my biggest faults is that I can't resist an adventure, and Duke knew it. After throwing on some clothes, I popped the screen on my window and crawled into the catalpa tree.

fourteen

DUKE'S PALS

We quickstepped through town, cutting across backyards and down alleys. If there was a streetlight, we shied away from it. We were barked at plenty but for once Duke held off on barking back. The late hour and growing storm kept everybody inside, and we reached the river without setting off any alarms.

We stopped at a clump of river birch, where a dugout canoe was tied up. The boat looked more log than ship, with a roughly chopped-out inside and a couple of stick paddles laid across it.

"It's perfectly safe," Duke said, his tone daring me to squawk.

"You first," I countered.

The storm was breathing down our necks by then, and to my surprise Duke did an un-Duke-like thing. He climbed aboard without arguing or calling me a wimp or threatening to dunk me. Wherever we were headed, he wanted to get there before the storm broke.

He was lying about the boat, of course. A block of ice wouldn't have been any tippier, or as fast. It skimmed across the water like a flat stone sent skipping. Cracked clamshells covered its floor, and the stink of dead fish rose from beneath the shells. A sticky goo had been smeared on the seats.

We pushed off, pointing toward the sloughs north of town, on the Minnesota side of the river. Thunder rumbled up and down the valley now, sounding like a stampede headed our way. I still couldn't see any lightning bolts, though at times they lit up sections of the sky a pink that was pretty as taffy but worrisome too. Once the storm hit we'd have to get off the water or take a chance on being barbecued.

Somehow the night found a way to get darker. Early on I saw a flashlight working along the riverbank and almost called out, "Dad," but Duke cut away from it before I had a chance. After that, the zigzags he took veered far from roads and cars and houses and anything with lights. We snaked through a maze of waterways where the trees hung low and lilies choked the path.

Finally, a bonfire appeared, all green and sparky, and it occurred to me that maybe Duke actually knew where he was headed.

There was singing. Squeaky brakes had it all over that singing. Shapes were dancing, or maybe stumbling.

We were almost to the bonfire when the first thunderbolt nailed the valley. My ears rang like gongs, and for a second everything looked bright as two high noons smushed together. During that blinding flash, the dancers' shadows dwarfed everything. Even the fire snapped and jumped as if trying to scramble away from them. It couldn't, though. And the shadows weren't anywhere near as dreadful as the dancers themselves.

"Trolls?" I gasped.

Even though I'd been expecting something of the sort, the hairs on the back of my neck stood at attention anyway.

"River trolls," Duke corrected, terribly proud of himself.

Whatever they were, they looked awfully glad to see us.

fifteen

CHUG·GA·LA·KA

We squeezed introductions in before the storm hit. They were called Stump, Biz, and Jim Dandy. Duke beamed as if they were the grandest names in the world.

They dressed like bicyclists, wearing yellow and blue nylon trunks and shirts, with a shiny smoothness that clashed with their rough scales. The way they strutted, you could tell they thought fashion couldn't get any higher than tight-fitting nylon. No helmets, no shoes, no gloves. Hard heads, webbed feet, long claws. Two of them had several inches on Duke. The one named Stump may have stopped a full head shorter than Duke but spread much broader.

Jim Dandy and Biz were frog green, and Stump leaned toward mud gray, though probably because he'd been rolling in something. Leafy willow-branch hair fell to their shoulders. Teeth, oh yes. Their stubby tails must have made sitting down a challenge. Their speckled scales had yet to sprout warts, the way old trolls supposedly do, though they weren't kids either. From everything I'd heard, trolls lived for hundreds of years, and didn't this bunch look it. And smell it. The log canoe I'd just climbed out of was perfume in comparison.

It seemed strange, but after a minute or two of gawking, I sort of got used to their snouts and knobs. In fact, it almost seemed as if maybe I'd spied them somewhere before, in a dream or video game or passing car. They weren't quite as scary after that thought. The red silk scarf around Jim Dandy's neck seemed almost silly, until he started to talk.

"So this is the cousin you promised?" Jim Dandy stood with an arm around Duke's shoulder, friendly as Duke was whenever he had his eye on something of mine.

"As promised," Duke bragged. "As promised."

All three of the trolls, plus Duke, gave me a close inspection then. Hard as Duke was checking, you'd have thought he'd never seen me before now. As for the troll eyes looking me over—they flashed orange as goldfish.

"She's kind of runty," Jim Dandy observed.

"Depends who's measuring," I said right back.

Jim Dandy had a good hoot over that, but the storm cut him short, blowing in with a crash and a blaze. Then the rain galloped in, and I felt as though I were caught in a car wash without a car.

The campfire climbed even higher in the downpour, which meant these trolls knew a little more about magic than keeping back doors open and turning people to stone. Too bad they didn't know a spell to keep their guests dry. The deluge started them dancing again, possibly in celebration, as around and around the campfire they whirled, bumping into each other and tossing puff balls on the blaze, which made the fire greener and higher.

Duke whirled too. In between lightning strikes, when you couldn't see as much, his horn let him fit right in with the crowd.

They howled a song as they danced. It's not the kind of song I hope to hear again anytime soon.

Chug-ga-la-ka, chug-ga-la-ka, spoon spoon
We dance in the dark
Not under the moon.

Chug-ga-la-ka, chug-ga-la-ka, hey hey
Lions and tigers
Get out of our way.

After a few verses I began to get the idea that they were trying to talk themselves into doing something brave, and that maybe, on the inside, they weren't so big and tough and scary after all.

Then, fast as the storm had arrived, it blew over. A carpet of clear, starry sky unrolled behind it, and the trolls turned sentimental. One of them, the one named Stump, pulled a ukulele out of an alligator-hide bag and started strumming a mournful tune. You'd have thought somebody's hamster had died. The troll called Jim Dandy started singing. It sounded as though he was having a tooth pulled, but Duke, standing respectfully off to the side, looked as though it was the prettiest tune he'd ever heard.

Goodbye, dear sisters,
We're leaving this river.
Goodbye, dear sisters,
We'll dig up our dads.

Our mothers don't want us—
We've turned truly rotten.
They drove us away
With the stone and the pan.
But someday they'll know

> How poorly they judged us
> When we come back
> With pure gold in our hands.
>
> Goodbye, dear sisters,
> We're leaving this river.
> Goodbye, dear sisters,
> We'll dig up our dads.
>
> We'll sniff up some stars
> And trade them for crickets,
> Whose lies will lead us
> Through sand and through fog.
> And when we find out
> The place our dads went to,
> We'll smash all their kettles
> And drink up their grog.
>
> Goodbye, dear sisters,
> We're leaving this river.
> Goodbye, dear sisters,
> We'll dig up our dads.

Every word of it was heartfelt and left me wishing there were some way I could help ease their sorrows. When the one called Stump wiped a tear from his eye and waved for me to join in, I gave Jim Dandy some help with the chorus.

> There's sure to be plenty
> Of cold porridge and glory.
> There's sure to be
> Treacherous times that are bad.
> But we don't fear nothing

Unless it's the story
Of Bo the Great Rock Troll
Who tricked all our dads.

Goodbye, dear sisters,
We're leaving this river.
Goodbye, dear sisters,
We'll dig up our dads.

We sang long enough for the moon to come up, yellow as a cat's eye and thin as someone who can't quit dieting. As soon as the moon arrived, Jim Dandy stopped singing and whipped out sunglasses, though in this case I suppose they should be called moonglasses.

Biz started to say something to Jim Dandy, then caught Duke listening and thought better of it. Grabbing a lock of Jim Dandy's willow hair, he yanked him off to the side for privacy. Jim Dandy went along without a squawk, which said tons about who really ran the show.

Duke leaned their way, eavesdropping for all he was worth. He couldn't have been hearing much, though, not the way his face was screwed up around his horn. Whatever he was missing left him plenty worried.

sixteen

SILVER DOLLARS

While Biz was roughing up Jim Dandy, the one named Stump eased up beside me to whisper, "Don't worry yourself any. I won't let them do anything real bad to you."

Of the three trolls, Stump was probably the ugliest, with whiskers that were bent and broken, and a bobbing Adam's apple. The tip of his snout, right around the nostrils, had a green duckweed foam bubbling out with every breath. But when he spoke, he sounded polite, protective, maybe a little simple, and, believe it or not, almost sweet.

"You mean like being turned to stone?" I said.

"Stone's not bad." The suggestion that it was surprised him. "Stone's nice and soothing. No, I'm talking about something like turning you into a church bell. Think how terrible that would be."

"Can you do that?" I asked. "Turn people into church bells, I mean."

"Not that I know of," Stump said with a startled laugh. "I was just saying it. You know, one of those for-example things."

I was about to ask how they turned people into stone, but Stump suddenly stiffened and shuffled away. Looking up, I saw Biz shoving Jim Dandy back toward the fire.

"Let's get down to business here," Jim Dandy barked, having

received his marching orders. "We need to get these screens by to-morrow night."

"Relax, boys," Duke advised, all chummy. "My cousin can get you screens, no problem. Maybe a bucket of willow cats too."

"Lip smackers?" Stump perked up.

Willow cats are a baby catfish that bait shops around here sell. They're not my idea of a tasty snack, but with thoughts of stone statues and church bells filling my head, I played along, hoping that Duke knew what he was doing.

"Screens first," Jim Dandy insisted, after a sharp poke from Biz.

"You've got to have a few nibblies on the way," Duke said, always on the lookout for his stomach, "or the trip's not worth making."

"But what if there's not enough money for both?" Jim Dandy pointed out.

The nervous way he mentioned it made both Biz and Stump's snouts jerk up, as if they'd just caught a whiff of something foul.

"Well," Duke griped, backing off a bit, "I suppose you're right about that, but I don't see what a treat or two can hurt."

"No," Stump moaned, disappointed, "got to be screens first."

Biz continued his silent ways. Instead of talking, he crossed over to an alligator bag and dug out a silver dollar that glinted in the fire-light. Stump got a dollar from another bag. Jim Dandy didn't budge, his grin growing suspiciously bigger.

"Where's yours?" Stump poked Jim Dandy's arm.

"Well, boys," Jim Dandy gushed, "I've been meaning to talk to you about that."

"You told us you stole one from your mother," Stump said.

"Now, you boys know how my mother is." Jim Dandy stepped away. "She's not the sort to leave her purse unguarded."

"But there's screens to buy." Stump was dumbfounded.

Biz took a threatening step forward.

"Now, boys," Jim Dandy cooed, holding his hands up for Biz to stop where he stood, "ain't I the one who spotted old Duke here and brought him on board? Oughtn't that be worth something powerfully good before this business is through?"

Duke nodded yes as fast as he could to that. It slowed Stump a bit too, though not Biz, who was busy reaching for a fresh handful of Jim Dandy's hair.

"And I'm willing to bet," Jim Dandy sped on, leaning away from Biz's grasping hand, "that Duke's little cousin here can get us three screens for two dollars."

"But screens have always been a dollar apiece," Stump protested, shocked at the notion that they could be had for less.

Biz glared without bothering to agree.

"Yes, they have," Jim Dandy said, doubling up on agreeable, "but you've heard how sweet this little cousin of his can sing. And if she can't get us three screens tomorrow, plus some willow cats, then I'll swim back home and pinch a silver dollar from my mother's purse, no matter what."

"You said that before." Stump frowned.

"And this time I mean it," Jim Dandy promised.

During the face-off that followed, I decided it was now or never and told Jim Dandy, "I could get you a silver dollar."

"She's got a heart of gold," Jim Dandy cried out with a laugh that didn't sway anyone, not even Duke, who was reaching for my ears.

"Matter of fact" — I grunted, twisting away from Duke — "I can get you three silver dollars. One for each of you if you'll just promise to take me and Duke home, and do something about Duke's parents and some others, like our grandpa, who made the mistake of touching them." They all looked at me with such blank faces that I felt obliged to add, "They're all stone."

"Don't promise her anything." Duke pointed an awfully thick

finger at me. "I'm not going home, and I like my parents the way you left them. And don't worry about silver dollars—I'll make her fork 'em over."

"What'd I tell you?" Jim Dandy patted Duke on the back like a proud father.

Biz drew a finger across his throat, shutting Jim Dandy up fast.

"Save your dollars," Stump muttered to me, downcast. "They wouldn't do us any good. These screens got to be bought with silver stolen from our mother's purses. Otherwise we'll never find our fathers."

"We don't know that for sure," Jim Dandy cautioned.

"Rules got to be followed," Stump said stubbornly. "Why do you think they're rules?"

Jim Dandy didn't come up with a slick answer for that, not with Biz trying to throttle him. It left me in a pretty tight pickle too, seeing as how I didn't have a backup plan to the silver dollars.

"Sit down," Duke growled in my ear. "Shut up."

He grabbed my arm too, but the instant he touched me his horn shot out another inch and he let go of me with a yelp. After that he left me alone, as we listened to the trolls carry on about how Jim Dandy was afraid of his own mother. They kept it up all the way to dawn, when they wrapped everything up in a hurry. Snatching their alligator bags, Stump and Biz each slapped a silver dollar in my hand.

"Talk sweet." Jim Dandy offered advice instead of a dollar.

"Don't worry," Stump said, doing enough of it for all of us.

As for Biz, he gave me a look so cold that it made me wish I were on my way, but I wasn't. Planting my feet, I announced that I wasn't going anywhere until they promised to change Duke's parents, our grandpa, and a couple of others back from stone.

Duke pretty near fainted from embarrassment, his cheeks boiled so red, but Jim Dandy only threw back his head and brayed loudly. It was Biz who gave me an answer.

"Done."

It was the first word I'd heard him say, and it answered why he was so willing to let Jim Dandy gab away. His voice was as high and squeaky as a baby bird's. Being a tough guy with a voice like that had to be all uphill. The way he held a paw out to shake on our deal wasn't exactly reassuring, not as grim as he looked, but I shook his scaly mitt anyway. Without a lawyer handy to draw up a contract, what could it hurt?

A couple of minutes before sunrise, they slid into the river. Biz led the way, followed by Jim Dandy, followed by Stump. Single file, they disappeared under the current. A few bubbles, then nothing, unless you counted a big bass jumping out of the water as if chased.

About then the sun popped up huge and red over the eastern bluffs like something was chasing it too. The campfire snuffed out, leaving a sickly green curl of smoke.

"Aren't they great?" Duke asked me.

seventeen

THE TRIP TO BIG ROCK

Duke hustled me back to the dugout canoe and slapped a paddle in my hands. When I asked how he knew where to go, he said, "They sent me over there yesterday, to arrange things."

My ears perked up at that, for Duke never explained anything unless trying to cover up something else.

"How'd they arrange to turn your folks to stone?" I pried, dipping my paddle into the river.

By daylight, I saw that the paddle was a crooked old stick with a flattened coffee can knotted to one end, but one stroke sent us skimming over the water. Duke's mood brightened with my question, so I knew that wasn't what he was hiding.

"Touched them with a feather," he bragged.

"What kind of feather?"

"There wasn't exactly time to ask. The back door blew open and there they were. It was really something."

Hoping to cut short his smirk, I tossed out, "So what'd you arrange at this store?"

"Never mind about that," he said, souring fast. "Just say you're there for screens."

When I pushed him on it, he got prickly, but I stuck with it until

he admitted that the store owner had refused to sell screens to anyone with a horn. Afterward, Biz had wanted to ditch him. When
Jim Dandy stood up for him, he pretty much made himself a friend
for life, no questions asked. It must have been about then that my
services got volunteered for free.

"What makes you think I'll have any luck getting screens?" I
asked.

"Not now," Duke grumbled under his breath. "They might be listening."

"Who?"

"Jim Dandy and the boys."

"Where?" I twisted about without glimpsing one troll snout in
the water.

Duke glared and dipped his chin toward the bottom of the canoe. I couldn't spot any trolls swimming beneath us either, but that
didn't mean anything, not muddy as the river was.

We paddled upstream toward Big Rock, a small village on the
Wisconsin side, and steered clear of the boat and barge traffic on
the main channel. It was a five-star spring day, blue and clear, and
more blue, and warm. Tree branches remained bare but you could
smell spring cooking inside them. It was too grand a day to waste
chasing around in a dugout canoe that was attracting the first flies
of the year.

"Say I help you with these screens," I said, keeping my voice low,
"then what?"

"We do some mining."

"With screens?"

"We'll need them for sifting sand."

"For what?"

"Stars."

He spit that out as if every doorknob in the world knew that much.

"I'm sure you'll find tons of them." I didn't even bother to roll my eyes. "What about your parents and Grandpa B?"

"Who cares?" Duke jeered.

Figuring he was trying to impress his new friends, I ignored that crack. "So we get these stars, then what?"

"We trade them to Bo the Great Rock Troll."

"The one who tricked their dads?" I remembered the trolls' song. "Are they going to make you an honorary troll for helping?"

"Maybe," Duke said, doing his best not to sound hopeful. A moment latter he gruffly added, "Hold on."

We shot across the main channel a quarter-mile before Big Rock and tied up below some railroad tracks. There was a nice dock right in town, but Duke refused to go anywhere near it. Turning sullen, he muttered that yesterday a bunch of kids on the dock had made fun of his nose. If he saw them again, he might tear them into little pieces, and we didn't have time for that. We were after screens.

"Get 'em and come back," he ordered, meaning no dilly-dallying.

"What if I need some help carrying them?"

"Figure it out."

"I might drop them."

"Don't."

He was about to add one of his famous or elses, but two large bubbles surfaced, popping near the boat. I caught a whiff of trolls.

"If you need help," Duke said, changing his tune fast, "stand on the end of the dock and wave."

"You're a peach." I scrambled out of the dugout before he could sock my shoulder, the way he usually did whenever I brought up peaches.

eighteen

TROLLS & THINGS

The village of Big Rock was wedged between the river and the base of the limestone bluff it was named after. The few houses were packed close together like sticks of gum. I was supposed to hunt up a store called Trolls & Things, which on a Sunday morning would probably be the only store open. The three other stores in town—Shop 'n' Go, Big Al's Everything, and New Antiques—took the day off.

An old silver bell jingled when I opened the heavy front door to Trolls & Things. After the bell, shadows and quiet greeted me. The store smelled like fresh rain, though it was perfectly dry, outside and in.

"Hello," I called out.

No one helloed back. A quick tour took me past wooden barrels that held yardsticks, square-toed boots, glass eyes, old trumpets, underwater wristwatches, and unmatched orange tennis shoes. Each barrel had an ALL SALES FINAL sign. And that was only a sampling of what I saw. To get anywhere, you had to walk sideways down aisles so narrow you brushed against nylon bicycle outfits, Christmas tinsel, Halloween masks, moonglasses, and potted ivy. Even the ceiling, high above, was crowded. Ukuleles hung from every rafter.

At the back of the shop I found three bathtubs filled with running water and minnows, suckers, shiners, and—especially—willow cats. A sign above the tubs said ALL SALES COMPLETELY FINAL!!!

"Hello-o," I called out again.

This time I got an answer, sort of.

A raccoon's masked face peeked out a door off to the side, hanging upside down from the door frame for an instant before ducking away. A minute later I heard footsteps.

"I'm coming, I'm coming," a familiar voice called out.

A moment later the old lady who had saved me at the wagon wheel bridge stepped through the door where the raccoon had been. She was wearing a different dress, a yellow flowery one this time, but the same straw hat and checkered apron and orange high-top tennis shoes. One of her tennies squished river water with each step. The raccoon played peekaboo from behind her skirt.

"Oh, it's you," the old lady said, friendly as ever. "Your cousin found you, then. I got your note and told him you were looking for him when he was in here nosing around yesterday." She chuckled when she mentioned Duke's nose but got serious again in a hurry. "There isn't much chance of him doing any good deeds while hanging out with Jim Dandy and his bunch." Clearing a stack of pointy black hats off a stool, she motioned for me to have a seat. "I suppose they sent you in here for screens."

"How'd you know that?" I frowned.

"Because Jim Dandy and his pals are about to become fathers. There should be a troll hatch any night now. The first new moon of spring is the time."

"What's that have to do with screens?"

"If you're doing errands for them," she supposed, eyeing me carefully, "I guess you've a right to know. They're under a curse, a pretty good one, actually. Nice and simple, the way a curse should be. If a river troll doesn't bring Bodacious Deepthink a shooting star before his firstborn is hatched, he gets turned into a human."

"That's a curse?" I was more than a little outraged to hear it.

"If you're a river troll, it is."

"Bodacious who?" I asked.

"Deepthink. Otherwise known as Bo the Great Rock Troll. It's her curse."

"What kind of human?" I spoke slowly, trying to think if I knew anyone who might qualify.

"Why, the same kind as you."

"So how come I've never seen one?"

"Oh, you wouldn't notice them." My suspicions amused her. "They're born in a hospital, same as any other baby. They don't even know where they come from themselves, except maybe deep down, where they don't quite feel as though they ever fit in. Even their mothers don't know." The raccoon tugged on her skirt, and the old lady leaned over to hear a whispered secret. "Princess Trudy thinks I might be scaring you."

"Maybe a little," I admitted.

"Well, I wouldn't worry about it too much," the old lady comforted. "A troll going human's a rare thing. Your average river troll can't stand the thought of washing with soap and eating vegetables all his life. Scares them silly. So they bring Bodacious Deepthink stars and clear out to look for their fathers as fast as they can."

"I see." Really, I felt blind. "Do you know anything about people who've been turned to stone?"

"Oh, dear," she fretted. "Who?"

"My grandpa, among others."

"Dear, dear. Your grandpa's much too lively a fellow to like being stone."

"You know Grandpa B?"

"Only since he was a boy."

nineteen

TALKING SILVER

Since you can hardly lift a rock around here without some story about Grandpa B crawling out, I wasn't totally surprised that the old lady knew him.

"Well," I said, "my cousin claims they turned his parents into stone with some kind of feather. Does that sound right?"

"Oh, yes. That's just what a stone feather would do."

"Thought so." I nodded, trying hard to act like an old river hand, even though I'd never before heard so much as a whisper about this kind of rivery business. "So when Grandpa went charging in and touched Duke's parents—more stone."

"Sounds like your grandpa," she agreed, "but he should have known better."

"He got pushed."

"Why, that's terrible," she said. "Is that why you're helping them out? So they'll turn them back?"

"Something like that." All of a sudden I went teary despite myself.

"There, there," she soothed. "You'll just have to get ahold of something they want really bad and trade it for the feather."

"I tried silver dollars—they weren't interested."

"Any other time they would have been," she assured me, "but

those boys are about to pay Bodacious Deepthink a visit. That means they're only interested in silver that can buy them screens."

"I know, I know," I said wearily. "And it's got to be silver from their mothers' purses."

"I'm afraid so. You'll just have to bide your time and keep your eyes open for something else to trade them. And whatever you do, don't let them trick you into touching the feather unless you're wearing a stone glove. Touch it without one and you're a goner."

"A stone glove?" I repeated, blinking.

"They'll have one around somewhere," she said, patting my arm reassuringly. "They couldn't hold the feather without it. That's about all I can tell you, I'm afraid, except that if you find yourself in a pinch, throw a riddle at 'em. That should at least buy you some time. If they were rock trolls, I'd say a riddle would be sure-fire. Rock trolls can't ever turn down a chance to prove how smart they are. River trolls are generally smarter than that, but they'll often as not bite on a riddle too."

"I'll try to remember," I promised.

"Good. As for Jim Dandy and his bunch, they're lucky I'll sell you any screens. They broke in here the other night and stole three ukuleles."

"I saw them playing just one." I was trying to be helpful.

"I stole the other two back." She winked. "And I'll get that third one too, if Bodacious doesn't get it first. Oh, don't look so surprised. It's not the ukulele she cares about: it's young river trolls. She tries to make miners out of them, which is what started all this nonsense in the first place. A long time back, Bodacious hired three river trolls to help her mine to the moon. They were never seen again."

"The moon?" I'm afraid my mouth was hanging open. "How can you dig a mine to something in the sky?"

"Better not let Bodacious Deepthink hear you say that," she

warned, raising a finger to her lips. "As far as she's concerned, when the moon sets, it sinks into the earth. You see, rock trolls believe that long, long ago the moon was their home. When it rises at night, they get misty-eyed just looking at it. Bodacious has staked her whole reputation on getting them back there, and nothing matters more to a rock troll than reputation."

"I had no idea." I swallowed hard. "But what happened to the missing miners?"

"Nobody knows. Bo claims she paid each of them a lucky cricket and sent them home, but the only ones who ever made it home were the crickets."

"What do they say happened?"

"Who knows? Bo keeps the crickets locked away, except when trading for shooting stars. Of course the three river trolls' wives retaliated by dulling Bo's picks and shovels with a curse. Bo didn't waste any time dreaming up a curse of her own. Back and forth they went, until the river trolls came up with a doozy: Bo will never find the moon until the three missing river trolls find their way home. Bo topped them, though: Any river troll who won't help mine has to bring her a shooting star to light the tunnel going to the moon, and he has to do it before the hatch of his firstborn. If he does that, fine, she trades him one of the crickets who knows where the first three miners went. If they don't . . ."

"They become human?" I cringed.

"Exactly. It's a possibility that curls their tails good. Once they're human, the only way to change back to a troll is to stand up to Bo in person, and so far as I know, it's never been done. So you'd better hand over their three silver dollars and go tell that cousin of yours to stay as far away from Bodacious Deepthink as he can manage."

"What would she do to him?" I asked.

"Put him on her pantry shelf, I shouldn't be surprised."

"I'm afraid they've only given me two silver dollars to trade," I confessed, not wanting to think about pantry shelves. "I'm supposed to use my sweet voice to talk you into a third."

"That's Jim Dandy for you." She clucked her tongue in disgust.

"Does the third dollar absolutely have to be from a troll mother's purse? What if I promised to sneak one out of my mother's? I doubt that she'd mind."

"Sorry," she firmly said. "Got to be from a river troll mother. I give each of them a silver dollar for her newborn boy, as a promotional for the store. Baby girls get free thornbushes. When the boys grow up, they bring the dollar back for a screen. The girls trade their thornbushes in for a look into the future. That's the going price."

"There must be exceptions," I reasoned. "I mean, what if a mother loses her silver dollar? Then what?"

"These silver dollars don't get lost," she explained, sounding awfully sure of it. "They're special."

She meant it too, wouldn't budge a bit, not even on a couple of free willow cats for goodwill. So I handed over the two silver dollars. They'd no more than touched the old lady's hand than the woman engraved on the first silver dollar started yapping away. I could see her lips moving as she said to the old lady:

"They've got your ukulele, you know."

"There's a rhino boy too." The woman on the second silver dollar chimed in.

"Several people have been turned to stone."

"A dog too."

"And they've been singing that ridiculous song."

"Chug-ga-la-ka, chug-ga-la-ka."

Quick as she could, the old lady dropped them in a nearby cookie jar and closed the lid, confessing sheepishly, "Helps keep me abreast of the troll community."

So now I knew why it had to be silver dollars from their mothers' purses or nothing at all. Such goings-on left me pretty much speechless and a touch numb. Talking silver dollars weren't something you ran into every day, not even along the river.

Collecting two screen doors, which were twice my height and wide as my hands could reach, I started edging out of the store.

Before I'd gone three steps, the old lady stopped me to take a hard look into my eyes, just the way she'd done in the rowboat.

"What do you see?" I whispered.

"A turtle," she answered, puzzled.

"Is it Lottie?" Suddenly I felt hopeful.

"Hard to say."

"What's she doing?"

"Hiding in her shell."

That didn't sound like Lottie, unless she was in trouble. Up to then I'd been avoiding the old lady's eyes by gazing above her head, but now, worried about Lottie, I lowered my vision.

My own reflection wasn't gazing back from her eyes. No, facing me was a young woman from another time. I say from another time because she was dressed in an old-fashioned frilly blouse and long skirt and sunbonnet that hid most of her face. Still, she struck me as kind of familiar, and after a while I thought maybe I knew why. I guessed the old lady was somehow showing me what she looked like way back when she was my age. If that was the case, she must have been even older than I'd thought, for the young woman peering out at me was dressed like a pioneer. Since my mom had drummed into me that you never, ever inquire about a lady's age, I asked instead what was so interesting in my eyes.

"An old friend," she sighed, sounding kind of happy and sad all at once.

twenty

THE GETAWAY

I made it out of Trolls & Things without knocking anything over, a miracle considering how heavy and awkward the screens were. Afraid that I'd trip and poke a hole in one, I headed to the town dock to wave for my cousin.

The two kids fishing off the dock caught the jitters as soon as they spotted me coming, as if maybe they'd seen screens come down that dock before. And once they saw Duke sprinting toward the dock in the dugout, one of them broke for town, shouting, "Rhino boy! Rhino boy!" The other tried pulling his minnow bucket out of the river. The trouble was, the bucket was too heavy with water for the little squirt to lift it by himself. Duke reached the dock before the kid could make a run for it.

"Where's the willow cats?" he asked, panting and looking behind me as if I'd left them somewhere.

"Couldn't get them."

"Jim Dandy wanted willow cats."

"He's lucky I got him two screens."

"Two!" Duke cried. "You know we need three."

All this time the kid pulling up on the minnow bucket was also doing his best to be invisible. It didn't work. Duke pointed at him and shouted, "You! What's in that bucket?"

"N-nothing," the boy squealed, stumbling backwards. He was a chicken-legged little kid, a redhead like Duke, but that didn't save him.

"Mine now!" Duke bounded onto the dock and jerked the rope out of the boy's hands.

By then a crowd was gathering at the end of the dock, so Duke didn't have time to unknot the minnow bucket's rope. From an inside pocket, he whipped out a jackknife and cut the bucket free of the piling it was tied to. The instant my cousin cut the rope, he let out such a yowl that I thought he'd sliced his hand. Then I saw that it wasn't his hand but his nose that was hurting. It was having another growth spurt.

Duke's howls attracted even more kids, and as their number grew, so did their bravery.

"In the boat," Duke shouted at me between yelps. "In the boat."

I tossed the screens across the dugout and jumped after them, landing up front. The dugout tipped without flipping.

"Paddle!" Duke yelled, diving in back with the bucket. "Paddle!"

I paddled. A good thing too, because I was the only one doing it. Duke held his nose with one hand and had his other hand curled around the minnow bucket as if protecting a cookie jar. We were halfway across the channel before picking up any speed.

Back on the dock, kids were throwing rocks and shouting. There were splashes in the water but no direct hits, so except for Duke's nose, it was a clean getaway. Duke didn't care about his nose, though. The minnow bucket was full of willow cats.

twenty one

MORE ABOUT DUKE'S HORN

We lazed about a sandbar all that Sunday, with nothing to do but sleep, argue, and hang low until nightfall, when we were supposed to hook up with the river trolls again. I asked Duke why he hadn't bothered to mention who ran Trolls & Things. He claimed he hadn't wanted to scare me. I brought up the stone feather. He threatened to pound me into pudding.

"I doubt your new friends will want me pounded into anything," I said.

"Once we find their fathers?" He cackled. "They won't care a bit."

Around noon an old couple in a houseboat pulled up to our sandbar, and Duke ordered me to create a diversion. He planned on stealing their lunch but got caught when his horn knocked over a pitcher of pink lemonade.

After getting past their amazement at Duke's nose, the old couple took pity, handing out hot dogs, potato chips, two fruit jars of lemonade, and radishes. They even sent along some complimentary packets of ketchup and mustard. Duke was willing to share only the radishes and mustard until his nose started to tingle — then he became unexpectedly generous.

By daylight you couldn't help but notice the changes to Duke's face: puffy, watery eyes; thickened lips; sunken cheeks; stretched ears; and, for some reason, thinning hair.

What's more, with all that horn, he had a hard time seeing in front of himself. That meant he was constantly turning his head one way or the other to get a good look at things. Afraid that he was about to crash his horn into something, he dared not run fast enough to catch me. I found that out when a blue heron flew overhead and dropped an orange tennis shoe in my lap.

"Give me that!" Duke squawked, lunging.

He missed, wide.

By then I was off and running. He was yowling, for as soon as he sprang at me, his horn acted up. The old couple tried comforting him, but he shrugged them off to chase me. I soon lost him on the back side of the island, where I plopped down against a huge cottonwood.

There were two pages inside the shoe, the first filled with Mom's handwriting:

> Claire,
> Help is on the way—I hope. A river troll by the name
> of Two-cents Eel-tongue visited me early this morning,
> which was how I found out you were gone. She's on the
> trail of her son, a troll named Jim Dandy, and believes
> he's with Duke. She promised three times to help you
> and Duke. An honest person probably would have only
> bothered to promise once, but she did at least offer to send
> this note. I offered her a silver dollar for your safe return.
> Love, Mom
> P.S. Your father and the sheriff are still searching. Don't let
> Duke talk you into anything.

The second page was a note from my older sisters:

> Claire,
> We put that toad of yours in the basement.
> Feeding time can wait for you.
> Lillie and Fran

The toad, whose name was Three, lived in a wool sock under my bed. No word of Lottie.

I had time enough to read the notes twice before hearing Duke crash through the underbrush. I popped the paper into my mouth and had both sheets swallowed before he sprang.

"What was in the shoe?" he demanded, grabbing the tennie and flinging it as far over the river as he could.

"Don't worry," I teased. "Help's coming."

"It better not be," he said, stomping off.

twenty two

COUNTING TO TWO

As soon as it got dark, we pushed off, searching for the trolls. Up the river we paddled, clinging to the shadows of the shoreline so that a barge wouldn't cream us.

Now that the ice was off the river, there was a steady flow of barges hauling grain and coal and gravel. Barges were the reason there were so many new sandbars. For the river to be deep enough to handle them, its main channel had to be dredged constantly. The sand dug up from the bottom had to be spit somewhere, and the closest place for spitting was the riverbanks. The sandbars grew higher with each season of dredging, some rising until as tall as trees or hills or office buildings. They went on and on and could have hidden anything from a small village to a pyramid.

We spotted the trolls' green campfire about a mile above Big Rock, on the highest sandbar yet. When we pulled into shore, Jim Dandy and Stump treated us better than royalty. Biz stood off to the side of the campfire, not yet ready to throw us kisses.

"What did I tell you?" Jim Dandy crowed when Duke held up the minnow bucket. "What did I tell you?"

"But how did he get them?" Biz asked, his voice squeaky but

stubborn, so stubborn that he no longer thought twice about talking in front of us.

"He stole it from a little kid," I tattled.

"I told you he had promise," Jim Dandy boasted.

"But did he make the kid cry?" Biz asked, not won over so easily.

"Big tears." Duke held his hands wide apart to show their size.

"He's lying," I told them.

"All the better," Jim Dandy answered with a laugh. "He's one of us for sure."

Even Biz couldn't help but smile a fraction then. Seeing that, Jim Dandy reached into the minnow bucket, pulled out a wiggling willow cat, and lobbed it over the fire to Stump. Before the shortest troll could drop the fish down his gullet, Biz recovered, saying, "Wait a minute. Let's count these screens."

Looking worried that Biz might make him put the fish back, Stump gulped it fast. At the same time, Duke stepped away from me, denying everything.

"It's her fault."

Instead of arguing, I took a half-step toward the shadows myself. I needn't have worried, though. The trolls didn't blame me for anything. Not yet, anyway.

They inched forward as though afraid of being bitten, but I soon saw that it wasn't the screens that scared them. It was counting the screens that had them buffaloed. For once, even Biz wasn't eager to get on with business. He crept forward, a quarter-step ahead of the others, but giving them plenty of chances to take the lead. Any time he waved Jim Dandy and Stump ahead, they came to a dead stop behind him.

"No, no, no." Stump wagged a finger.

"You're the one so big on counting," Jim Dandy said.

"Tadpoles," Biz mutter-squeaked under his breath.

So Biz reached the screens first, and after a half-dozen tries, he managed to run a trembling finger over their edges. He couldn't count beyond one, though. Actually, I'm not sure if he got that far, which made it the worst case of counting jitters I'd ever seen. Jim Dandy and Stump weren't any help either. They constantly distracted Biz by trying to peek over his shoulder.

"There's only two of them," I announced at last, tired of their stalling. "The old lady wouldn't give me any more, not even when I talked extra sweet."

"I knew it!" Biz squeaked triumphantly.

"Now, let's not get all excited." Jim Dandy made a calming motion with his hands.

"I'd say you better swim on home for another silver dollar," Biz replied, ignoring him.

"If you think I'm going to miss the new moon like Stump's fool brother did," Jim Dandy shot back, "you're dumber than driftwood."

That crack had Stump clenching his fists hard enough to juice apples. Biz wanted to snap back, you could tell by the way his stubby tail was twitching, but before he could answer, Jim Dandy went on smoothly.

"Besides, there's other ways to get that third cricket from Bo."

"Not tried-and-true ways," Biz squeaked.

"Relax, boys," Jim Dandy cooed. "I got you the ukuleles, didn't I?"

"He did do that," Stump remembered, unclenching his fists.

"Yes, and she got two of them back," Biz reminded everyone.

"Hey," Jim Dandy protested, "I got you Duke, didn't I?"

"He did that too," Stump cautiously agreed.

"What good's he done us?" Biz challenged, crossing his arms.

Duke got a real nasty look on his kisser when he heard that, the kind of look that sooner or later always gets him into deep trouble.

Since he wasn't saying anything sooner, I figured later was what he had in mind.

"He got us his cousin, didn't he?" Jim Dandy swept a hand toward me.

"We wouldn't have needed either of them," Biz squeaked, "not if we'd all gotten a silver dollar from our mothers."

"Let me ask you this," Jim Dandy said, changing the subject as fast as he could. "Have you ever thought about what happens if Bo has enough shooting stars?"

"She never has enough of those," Biz scoffed.

"How do you know?" Jim Dandy asked. "She might be sitting on her throne right now, thinking, 'It's way, way too bright in here. I'm tired of all these shooting stars.'"

"Never happen," Biz squeaked, but you could tell he wasn't absolutely certain about it.

"Never?" Stump echoed weakly.

"But what if she did say no?" Jim Dandy insisted. "Then what would we do? I mean, we'd still need the crickets, right?"

Such questions crinkled up Biz's forehead and made Stump's eyes wild. One look told you that according to all reports, Bodacious Deepthink had always been willing to swap a cave cricket for a shooting star. No one had ever suggested otherwise—until now.

twenty three

EATS

$\mathscr{C}$an't you get by without the crickets?" I asked.

"Impossible," Jim Dandy stated. "We've got to have them to find our dads. So the question I'm asking is this—what do we give old Bo if she says no to shooting stars?"

Both Biz and Stump scowled as if it was a trick question.

"Duke," Jim Dandy said, making my cousin jump. "You tell them."

"An IOU?" Duke suggested. He'd always been a firm believer in them, so long as he didn't have to pay them back.

"Bo doesn't take IOUs," Jim Dandy chided.

"Oh," Duke muttered, deflating fast.

"Duke's cousin?" Jim Dandy moved on to me without having bothered to learn my name. "What would you give her?"

"Something else?" I had no idea what he was fishing for.

"That's it!" Jim Dandy whooped.

"But what?" Stump said.

"What else do we know that she likes?" Jim Dandy prodded.

"Eats?" Stump guessed, inspired.

"She *is* a rock troll," Biz reluctantly agreed. "She'd be hungry."

"So there's your answer." Jim Dandy bowed. "If we come up

short on shooting stars, we offer her a feast she can't resist. And that's where our old friend Duke comes into the picture."

"I do?" Duke revived.

"He does?" Stump seconded, so surprised that his nostrils bubbled out some extra green froth.

"Indeed he does," Jim Dandy assured them, slapping Duke on the back in that especially friendly way he had. "We need someone to help us carry the eats."

"What kind of eats?" Duke sounded eager to please as a puppy.

"Oh, legs of mutton, wheels of goat cheese, a barrel or two of pigs' feet." Jim Dandy laid this out with a generous wave of his hand. "Some ox tails would go over big. The usual stuff that rock trolls gobble."

"Where are you going to get all that?" I asked. "You don't even have a dollar to buy a screen."

"Don't be so ignorant," Duke scoffed. "Trolls have their ways."

"Indeed we do," Jim Dandy agreed wholeheartedly. "And fine ways they are."

"She's going to want her stars," Biz stubbornly squeaked.

"But if she doesn't," Jim Dandy insisted, winking at me and Duke, "we've got a plan, right? So let's not worry our pretty little heads about shooting stars. Agreed?"

As Jim Dandy explained all this, Biz and Stump gazed toward the river, giving me the uncomfortable feeling that they couldn't bear to look Duke or me in the eye.

—twenty-four—
SNIFFING FOR STARS

Grandpa B always claimed that shooting stars were craters falling off the moon, though he had a twinkle in his eye whenever he said it. How many of them hit the ground? I don't imagine anyone knows for sure, but to find some of those that do touch down, you've got to look in the right places. It turned out that any place that was covered with trees and bushes and grass was the wrong place. When it came to shooting stars, plants hide things. That was why the trolls headed for the center of the sandbar, which was nothing but a huge sandbox, hardly a plant anywhere.

"Nose funnels are the only way to go," Jim Dandy lectured. Digging out a pair of small brass funnels from his alligator bag, he stuck them into his nostrils.

"Lot you know about it," Biz squeaked. "All you really have to do is clear your sniffer out good and clean so there's nothing between it and the aroma."

To prove his point, Biz pulled a small gold box out of his alligator bag. The box was filled with a moldy bluish powder, a tiny pinch of which he packed up his nostrils, one at a time. The sneezes that followed were like cannon blasts and bounced him backwards two hops.

"Rookies," Stump muttered, shaking his head to show how pathetic Jim Dandy and Biz's approaches were. From inside his alligator bag, he lifted out a wire cage and from inside the cage he coaxed out a teacup poodle, all done up in ribbons and frills and hardly bigger than a pocket-size teddy bear. After patting the toy-size dog gently on the head and whispering softly in its ear, he set it on the sand and called out, "Fetch!"

The poodle darted off into the night, with Stump grabbing a burning stick from the fire to chase after him. Jim Dandy and Biz grabbed torches and took off running too, snouts working hard. I tried a sniff or two myself, with no results other than to make Duke laugh.

"You haven't got the nose for it," he told me, and then, to prove he had, he stuck his nose straight up in the air and took one long, hard sniff. "Yup," he gloated. "They're out there."

"So what do they smell like?" I wanted to call his bluff.

"A little like a grilled cheese sandwich that's been burned." His nose twitched. "Only sweeter."

The sandbar we stood on rose as high as a good-size hill, with a crown that was as flat and large as a football field. Duke and I dragged the screens and other mining stuff up top and waited for instructions. It took several trips, and for once in his life Duke did most of the work. He didn't want me touching anything valuable, and when it came to his friend's mining equipment, most everything was priceless.

The night was dark and, so far, moonless. We wouldn't have been able to spy Jim Dandy, Biz, or Stump if they hadn't been carrying torches. By then I'd figured out that I was probably going to need help finding the stone feather and, unlikely as it seemed, Duke was my best bet. I started my campaign to win him over with a shot in the dark.

"So what's Jim Dandy promising you?"

"Nothing." Duke answered way too quickly.

"Whatever it is," I predicted, "he'll never deliver."

"Which proves that you don't know doodley about Jim Dandy Eel-tongue."

"I know his own friends don't trust him."

"They're river trolls," Duke shot back. "What'd you expect?"

"I don't think they brush their teeth either."

"Never." Duke was happy about that. "Don't floss either."

"How about cleaning up their rooms?"

"They don't have rooms."

"Go to school?"

"Unheard of." Duke grew happier by the minute.

"Sounds perfect," I said. "Think I could join up?"

Not that I had any intention of signing up, but I had to burst my cousin's bubble somehow. Wanting to tag along was tried-and-true.

"Not a chance," Duke cautioned, stiffening.

"What'd they say when you asked to join them?"

"Never mind about that," Duke growled.

He took such an active dislike to my questions that I naturally kept right on asking them.

"Maybe you could ask for me," I begged. "They'd probably listen to you."

"Look," Duke threatened, shaking a fist in my face, "we both know you brush your teeth twenty times a day and keep your room neat as a box of fancy chocolates, except for all the toads and turtles and stuff. So let's not pretend you actually want to be a troll. Okay? We both know that what you're really up to is finding out what Jim Dandy's promised me. Right?"

"True enough," I cheerfully admitted.

"All right, then." Duke checked over his shoulder to make sure we were alone, then spoke out the side of his mouth. "Jim Dandy says he can get me a second horn."

"That's all?" I knew there had to be more because Duke still wasn't looking me in the eye.

"And a tail."

"Whoopee."

"And maybe some hooves," Duke snapped, finally looking me square in the eye. "But not for sure on those."

"What do you want with all that?"

"If I'm going to run with river trolls," Duke said, "I'll need them."

I never got a chance to ask where he came up with that brilliant idea. Just then Stump came rushing up with his toy-size poodle in one hand and a burning stick in the other. A guilty look was slipping off his face.

twenty five

DUCKWAD

"Jim Dandy wants you," Stump relayed to Duke. "Over that way."

The troll waved toward the back side of the island, and Duke took off at a full gallop, no questions asked.

As soon as Duke was gone, Stump turned shy, but not so shy that he left me standing atop that sandbar all alone. He stood there petting the toy poodle and sneaking peeks at me.

"I suppose you're wondering about my brother?" Stump said at last, cranky and defiant at once.

"The one Jim Dandy mentioned?" I asked, feeling my way.

"That's right." Stump nodded slowly. "Duckwad was his name, and you can call him a fool, if you want. I don't mind that. But all that other bad stuff that trolls say, that don't belong on him. That's not called for. Uh-uh."

"What other stuff?"

"What other? Like his cutting little trolls' hair off when they sleep. Duckwad only got caught at that once. Said he'd never do it again. See? Far as I know, he kept that promise, except for maybe once or twice. Twice, maybe. And they said he tied fish tails together with string. Never did. I did that. He took the credit is all. See? And all that stuff about cheating at riddles? So what if he wasn't any good at 'em? Not every troll is. And so what if he liked to brush his teeth? Is that some kind of crime?"

"I see your point," I said.

By then Stump had forgotten all about being shy and was crowding me.

"Duckwad wasn't anywhere near so bad." Stump thumped a foot down. "He just never had any luck with them calendars. He got his months wrong. That's all. See? That's why he didn't go looking for our fathers in time. See what I'm saying? He thought March. It was April. See? He wasn't any coward."

"Are you saying he got turned into a human?" I asked, picking my words carefully.

"Yes," Stump sobbed. "That. It might work out for you, but it's worse than lightning bugs up the nose for us. And the stain don't ever leave the family. Ever. Burned right in. But it's not fair for everybody to go around looking down their snouts at us 'cause of some calendar Duckwad didn't have any luck with. Uh-uh. Call that fair? Huh?"

"Sounds like you miss him," I guessed.

With that, Stump stopped talking altogether and turned his back to me, acting as if a poodle hair had landed in his eye. Even his poodle saw through that and gave his big ugly snout a lick to cheer him up.

"I don't miss him at all," Stump sniveled, "not with all the dirty tricks he played on me. I just wish he'd known how to read a calendar, that's all."

"What if he stood up to this Bodacious Deepthink?" I said. "Isn't that supposed to bring him back?"

"So they say." Stump shrugged hopelessly. "But that will never happen. He's a human now and doesn't even know he needs to stand up to her. No, he's gone for good, but I didn't come here to boo-sa-hoo about Duckwad."

That sounded like two or three lies rolled into one. While he was delivering them, he stretched his neck up as high as he could and checked all around us, making sure we were alone. Lowering his voice, he whispered, "I came to say that you better take your cousin home."

He must have thought I was going to argue with him, because he wouldn't let me answer.

"Yes, home," he went on. "That's what I came for. To tell you that."

"You mean Jim Dandy doesn't need Duke anymore?"

"Jim Dandy can use all the Duke he can get," Stump warned. "But your cousin might want to keep all the Duke he can. He might need it. Things around here might not be so safe for any Dukes, so make him go. He don't belong here, that's all. Bodacious Deepthink takes one sniff of your cousin and . . . huh! I don't want to be thinking about that."

"I'm surprised you're telling me all this."

"Me too," Stump glumly admitted. "Helping out's a weakness of mine. My own sweet Mrs. is always saying it's so, but nobody bothered to tell my brother what was right. He was all the time hunting up shortcuts. Nobody said, 'Don't do that. Or that. Or that.' Maybe if somebody had, he might not be in the fix he's in. See? So you got to make your cousin go home. Working in Bodacious Deepthink's mines is worse than anything."

Didn't I feel small then? For even thinking I couldn't trust Stump, I mean. I was trying to figure out some way to thank him and also ask for their stone feather when a cannon blast stopped me cold. All of a sudden Stump could hardly catch a breath, and when he did manage to say something, his voice was raspy and low.

"Don't say nothing on me," he begged. "Please."

Of course the blasts hadn't been from a cannon but from Biz, sneezing. Clomping up to us, he planted his torch in the sand and said to Stump in a rushed squeak, "Jim Dandy wants you and that star hound of yours. He thinks he's on to something. Off that way."

And Biz pointed toward the back side of the sandbar, the same place Stump had just sent Duke.

KING BIZ MOSSBOTTOM

"What are you looking at?" Biz grunt-squeaked.

There wasn't much I could say, since I was staring straight at him. My loss of voice suited Biz fine, though, for he was in a mood to talk.

"I'll tell you what you're looking at," Biz said airily. Straightening up, he placed one foot slightly forward and tucked a hand behind his back. "You're looking at the future king of the river trolls, King Biz Mossbottom, the First." He lifted his chin in a noble pose. "I suppose that surprises you."

"Not at all," I answered, quick as I could manage.

"You're lying," Biz squeaked. "I've never met a one of you things from Blue Wing that's any good at lying."

If he was trying to pick a fight, he was on his own. In my politest voice, I said, "Sounds right. How are you going to become king?"

"Simple. By bringing back our fathers. All of them."

I nodded to show that I was keeping up with him so far.

"Step one is getting rid of your cousin," Biz squeaked. "Once he's gone, Jim Dandy will get serious about raiding his mother's purse for a silver dollar. There's still time to do things the way they're supposed to be done."

"Makes sense to me," I agreed. "How you going to shake Duke?"

"I'm not. You are. If I send him packing, Jim Dandy will get sulky and won't be worth anything. He learned all about the sulks from that wife of his, Fancy Leechlicker. Real muckety-mucks, those Leechlickers. But much as I hate to say it, I may need Jim Dandy's big mouth to do some talking before this is all done."

"What makes you think my cousin will listen to me?"

"Easy," Biz predicted. "Tell him that I said I will turn him into stone the first chance I get."

"That ought to help," I granted. Clearing my throat, I managed to add, "If you don't mind my asking, what about the people you've already turned to stone? When are you planning to undo them?"

"After we get our lucky crickets," he said, "there'll be plenty of time for that."

"How do I know that you'll do it?"

"I'm giving you the word of a soon-to-be king," Biz squeaked, outraged.

"Not enough," I bluffed.

"All right," Biz grumble-squeaked, backing off. "I'll give you something that will prove I mean business."

Turning to the stuff that Duke and I had lugged to the top of the sandbar, Biz dug out his alligator bag and rummaged around inside it. A greenish glow seeped out of the bag, and there may have been some singing inside the bag too, although it was faint and could have been coins or necklaces jangling against each other. Try as I might, I couldn't manage a peek over Biz's shoulder to see if there was a stone feather in there.

Whatever that bag held, there was a lot of it. None of it was packed too neatly either, not the way Biz was rooting around and gibbering, "It's got to be in here" and "Who threw that in?" and "No, not you." And all the time the squeak of his voice got higher, and higher yet, and tighter and tighter, until at last he found what he wanted and cried out in an extra-high, relieved voice, "Here!"

With both hands, he lifted out a crown, which he gently sat atop his head.

"I had this made for my coronation," he trumpeted.

"It's something," I acknowledged.

And it was. Three frog skins stood up on its front, covered in mold and slime that made my nose wrinkle. Dripping Spanish moss was draped over their shoulders like royal robes. They were standing on a headband made from skin that had once been cozy with a diamondback rattlesnake. The snake's rattles hung down between Biz's orange eyes, which were blazing.

"You can hold on to this," Biz decreed, "as collateral. Deal?"

"Deal," I echoed.

Lifting the crown off, Biz pushed down on its middle tine and said something that sounded sort of like a sneeze and sort of like saying "chicken noodle soup" real fast. In a twinkling, the crown shrank down to ring size.

"Put out your hand," Biz ordered.

I did and he slid the crown-ring on the middle finger of my left hand. It fit snugly and felt alive, turning this way and that as if the frogs were trying to see what was going on.

"You do your part," Biz squeak-pledged, "and I'll do mine."

"What if I can't convince Duke?" I asked, squeaking a bit myself. "He can be awfully stubborn."

"Then I'll want my crown back." He made it sound as though he'd take my finger too.

With that, Biz shoved me toward where he'd last seen Duke. I didn't get far, though, barely over the first dune. Someone hiding on the back side of it tripped me. When I looked up, I came face-to-face with a grinning Jim Dandy.

"Gave you his crown, did he?"

twenty seven

JIM DANDY EEL·TONGUE

I didn't squeal in surprise—couldn't, not with Jim Dandy's hand covering my mouth. His palm was surprisingly soft, though clammy.

"I wanted a word in private," Jim Dandy breathed in my ear.

When I nodded that I understood, he lifted his hand away and dropped an arm over my shoulder to let me know I wasn't going anywhere.

"I suppose Biz wants you to take Duke home," Jim Dandy said. "He's afraid your cousin will help me be the hero of this expedition, and truth be told, you probably wouldn't mind getting him out of here either. River trolls aren't the best of company for a boy and all that, even if he does have a horn and the start of a tail."

"What do you mean, 'tail'?"

"I shouldn't be surprised." Wanting to seem bored, Jim Dandy yawned for show. "The longer he runs with us, the likelier he is to sprout one, so I can see why you might want to get him home. Sooner the better, you're probably thinking. Well, if you're worried that I'll try to stop you, don't give it another thought. I'm behind you all the way on this one. For once, I'm thinking Biz is on to something."

"You are?"

"Oh, yes," Jim Dandy assured me. "I've come around to seeing that we all might be better off without Duke hanging around. I hate to say it — I mean, I love the guy and everything — but he's something of a loser. What I'm thinking is that there's somebody much better suited to take his place and help us get the crickets we need. By the way, that somebody's you."

Hearing that made me swallow wrong, which started me coughing. Jim Dandy whipped off his red scarf and used it to muffle my coughs.

"No need to thank me," he said. "I know you'll do everything you can to help us, what with all the stone in your family."

That was a threat, of course, and as soon as I was done coughing, I begrudgingly said, "I see what you mean."

"I thought you might. Now, why don't you share what Biz was telling you, and then we'll figure out what to do from there."

"Mostly, he talked about how he was going to be king."

"Bah!" Jim Dandy indignantly cried out.

Realizing he'd been too loud, he sneaked a peek over the dune to check on Biz's whereabouts. Reporting that Biz was gone, Jim Dandy slid his arm off my shoulder, saying, "Maybe I better straighten you out on a thing or two."

Feel free to believe about half of what follows. Maybe less.

"Did you know," Jim Dandy started out, "that Biz's mother was afraid she'd never get rid of him? She offered me money to let him come with me and Stump. Yes, I know, it doesn't seem right, but that's the way it is sometimes. He's twice as old as me and Stump, you know. That's because there's only one way to get around Bodacious Deepthink's curse, and that's to never get married and father a hatch. Bo's curse can't touch you then. And that's the way Biz was playing it too — up to last fall. That's when his mother locked him out of their lodge and wouldn't let him back in until he got married. It was getting cold. Ice was topping off the sloughs. It took all that to convince Squeak Mossbottom to get hitched."

"Squeak?" I blinked.

"That's what everybody really calls him. Biz is something he dreamed up. And who do you suppose he up and married?"

"I wouldn't have any idea."

"The Crowleg sisters," Jim Dandy snorted. "All three of them— Muck, Weed, and Scale. The Crowlegs have been trying to marry those girls off for a century or more. They're ugly and mean as a bag of leeches that's just been sat on, and the only thing pretty about 'em is their warts."

"If they're so bad," I asked, "why'd he marry them?"

"Their eyesight," Jim Dandy said with a shrug. "Most troll wives claim they can see an hour or two ahead. The Crowleg sisters say they've got eyes that can see a whole day into the future. Maybe that's what makes them so mean. Knowing Squeak, he probably thought they would give him an edge in finding our fathers. Only one problem there."

"What's that?"

"They're not here with us, are they? So they can't very well tell us what they can see. That's Squeak all over. Plan everything out a hundred different ways, then forget something so simple as that. And don't go thinking Stump's any better," Jim Dandy warned me. "His mother was so afraid that he'd turn out like his brother Duckwad that she begged me to take him along. They're mighty lucky to have me, those two are. I'm about the only chance they have to ever make it back. Stump's wife told them so too."

"How'd she know?"

"Wishy Gartooth?" Jim Dandy said. "She's been known to see clear into next week if the pay's good."

"So what'd she see?" I asked, not sure I wanted to know.

"Me, saving the day."

The crown-ring on my finger bit into my skin with that news, but I never let on it was pinching me.

"Now, listen up," Jim Dandy whispered, turning secretive. "Here's the deal I'll cut you. I nabbed this when I got the ukuleles . . ." Here he slapped a brass skeleton key in my hand. "Take it and head down to the old lady's shop for that third screen. It opens the back door, so you can slip in and out easy as a breeze. That old lady won't be none the wiser. And once you've got that screen for me, I'll take care of getting Duke running home."

"How?"

"Easiest thing in the world," Jim Dandy puffed. "I'll tell him *we're* going to drop him off the wagon wheel bridge if he doesn't quit tagging along. Yes, yes, we saw all that. And don't fret about those people we turned to stone. After we get our lucky crickets there'll be plenty of time to swing by and tickle them with the old stone feather. They'll be good as new." Pointing me toward the river, he said, "So you better get moving. The dugout's this way."

After escorting me a few steps, he snapped his nose funnels back in place and left me to it. The last I saw of him, he was loping on all fours, sniffing sand as he went.

The river wasn't a direction I was too keen on heading. After dark, floating logs aren't always floating logs, if you know what I mean. And paddling down a dark river in a troll boat that was as tippy as a leaf and as smelly as clam juice didn't sit too steady on my stomach. Breaking into the old lady's shop, considering how kind she'd been to me, didn't sit any better.

But I went. What other choices did I have? None that I could see, or at least not any that I could see until I was just about to step into the dugout canoe. At that very moment a river troll climbed out of the bushes to my left and declared, "Hold everything."

twenty eight

TWO·CENTS EEL·TONGUE

The troll who had come out of the bushes was a darkish blob about the size and shape of a door. How did I know it was a troll? The eyes. They did the usual orange dance. The smell of river-bottom muck was a giveaway too. Her hands were floating in front of her, ghastly-like, as if headed for my throat.

"Where do you think you're headed?" she barked.

There wasn't much doubt it was a she. Her voice, though snappish and bossy, was more musical than the other trolls', and a purplish glow on her claws seemed more ladylike than manly. She must have been older too, for she didn't wear the latest bicyclist fashions but a heavily patched wetsuit. Stopping five feet short of me, she gave me a good sniff and grumbled, "You could use a little dirt behind your ears."

"Yes, ma'am." I nodded politely. "And who might you be?"

"Jim Dandy's mother," she said. "Much as he'd like to forget it. Two-cents Eel-tongue by name."

"My mom wrote me about you," I said, more relieved than I cared to mention. "She said you might help with my cousin Duke."

"He the one with the horn?"

"I'm afraid so."

"Now, there's a boy with promise," she predicted. "Tell you what, you do one little thing for me, and I'll help you get your cousin home. I'll even give you some help with those stone people your mother seemed so worried about. Interested?"

"I am." I shivered.

"Take this screen to Jim Dandy."

That was when I realized she was holding a screen door between us. It'd been invisible in the dark but sure enough explained why her hands had seemed to be floating in front of her so funny and why she looked square as a door.

"Nothing more?" I was thinking trap.

"Simple as that," she promised. "Once they have three screens, they won't be needing you or your cousin. You'll be free to take off. And once they've used the screens and paid their visit to Bodacious Deepthink, they'll have plenty of time to de-stone those people, though why anyone would rather be human than stone is beyond me."

"What if I can't get my cousin to go?" I asked.

"That's your problem. With a boy like Jim Dandy, I've got headaches of my own. I've done my best to raise that little mud bubble right, so it's all his father's fault. He was a coward too. Some boys will steal from their mother's purse two or three times a week without having to be nagged a bit. Not Jim Dandy. Oh, no, I've been waiting years and years to catch him in there just once. And all the while I've had to listen to that silver dollar in my purse blabbing away about every little thing that boy's no good at. It's been a load, especially since he married a Leechlicker, and I don't mind saying so."

"Yes, ma'am," I agreed, "but what if your son still won't help with my grandpa and the others?"

"Oh, settle down," Two-cents Eel-tongue muttered, annoyed. "If you're so worried about that, all you have to do is make sure Bodacious Deepthink doesn't talk him into anything stupid."

"How am I going to do that?"

"Nothing to it. Go along with him. And if she does talk the little fool into something, I'll give you just the thing to fix it—a riddle. Guaranteed to drive Bodacious crazy or worse."

"Are you sure?"

"Absolutely. It should give Jim Dandy all the time he needs to come to his senses and slip away. He ought to be able to get at least that much right."

"Maybe so," I said. "But how can I be sure he won't just disappear after he slips away?"

"Stick with him. He'll need all the help he can get if he's going looking for that worthless father of his. Those so-called friends of his aren't any prizes. Now, do you want this riddle or not?"

"I guess so," I said, "if it's all you've got."

"Not so fast," Two-cents came back. "If I'm handing out riddles, I want another favor too. When you give Jim Dandy this screen, don't tell him you got it from me. Don't even tell him I was here. Say that you got it yourself, the way I heard him tell you to."

"Why?" I asked.

"'Why?'" she mimicked. "What do you think happens if I take it to him? I'll tell you what. His partners won't ever let him live it down. Bad enough I had to make their mothers promise that those boys would take Jim Dandy along. But it'd be worse yet if I showed up here. He'd probably run away and end up turned into a little girl like you, only cuter, of course, with pigtails and warts and frilly skirts."

"But wouldn't he be turned into a boy?" I asked.

"Boy or girl," she said, laughing, "it doesn't matter to Bodacious Deepthink's curse. Human's all she said. And I don't want that worthless son of mine to be either, though it'd serve him right, but his father's already given the riffraff along this river enough to gab about."

"Fair enough," I allowed, skipping over what Jim Dandy's father had done. "I never saw you. What's the riddle?"

Closing her eyes to concentrate, she recited:

> What dreams of red,
> Mines gold in veins,
> Makes a good stew,
> And always complains?

I had to ask her to repeat it twice, which she did with glee. Then I lipped it to myself several times, and all the while Two-cents Eel-tongue grew merrier and merrier.

"No one's ever solved this one," she said with a cackle.

"How do you know?"

"Because I just made her up."

I was about to ask her to repeat it one more time when someone started shouting on the far side of the island. Other voices soon joined in, all of them excited.

"They found one," Two-cents said, sounding almost proud.

For a second, she actually seemed like a mother. I didn't have time to dwell on it, though. Right away Duke started bellowing my name from the top of the sandbar.

"Claire!" Duke shouted. "Claire! You've got one minute to get up here. Or else!"

There went my last chance to solve the riddle.

"Take Jim Dandy this screen." Two-cents shoved it toward me. "Forget I was ever here."

"What about the riddle?" I reminded her. "What's the answer?"

"Leeches," she hissed, and with that she dove into the river without making so much as a ripple.

Leeches? I guessed you had to be a river troll to appreciate it.

twenty-nine

TUG OF WAR

Up the sand hill I struggled with the third screen door, Duke's mouth blazing above me all the while. Up top I found my cousin heaping mining equipment on his shoulders, all ready to push off without me, but as soon as he saw what I was holding, he dropped everything.

"Where'd you get that?" he demanded.

"Jim Dandy sent me for it," I answered, keeping my word to Two-cents Eel-tongue.

"Hand it over," he growled.

Snatching the screen, he sailed off toward the back side of the island, holding the screen above his head by balancing its middle bar on the tip of his horn.

I grabbed the torch that Duke had left behind and gave chase.

Finding the others wasn't a problem, not with the way they were squabbling about who'd found the shooting star first. Duke quieted them by galloping to the rescue with the screen.

"Here's the third screen." Duke gasped, all out of breath.

"Where'd you get that?" Biz squeaked, suspicious-like.

"What's that matter?" Duke griped. "It's a screen, isn't it?"

"Sure looks like a screen," Stump said, grinning kind of simply at Duke.

"There's more to you than meets the eye." Jim Dandy swatted Duke on the back. "And I've always said it. Now if you'll just give me that old lady's key . . ."

"You stole her key?" Biz shudder-squeaked.

"Borrowed," Jim Dandy corrected. "We'll take it back when we're done."

Here, Jim Dandy held a paw out for Duke to drop the key in, but of course the key was still in my pocket. Jim Dandy kept his hand out there, though, grinning as if he knew a secret. An embarrassed silence fell over us until finally I couldn't take it any longer and slapped the key in Jim Dandy's palm.

By then Duke looked ready to bawl, but Jim Dandy wiped away the tears by dropping an arm over my cousin's shoulder and applauding his efforts, "Stealing a little credit, are we? Couldn't have handled it any better myself. Duke, old boy, you're going to be one of us yet." Turning to Stump and Biz, he rubbed in his victory by saying, "I told you not to worry."

After that, Jim Dandy strutted around as if walking on stilts. The way he carried on about how nobody had trusted him to contribute his fair share—well, it went miles beyond shameless, and of course it didn't leave him any time to chase Duke away by threatening to drop him off the wagon wheel bridge. What finally shut him up was Biz, who interrupted to squeak, "What about this star?"

—thirty—
MINING FOR STARS

You two," Jim Dandy ordered, pointing at Duke and me, "help Biz and Stump haul the mining stuff over here."

"Hold on, now," Biz squeaked. "That'd leave you here all alone."

"Somebody's got to mark the spot," Jim Dandy said.

"Somebody," Biz agreed, "but not you."

"Nice try," Stump added.

There followed a whole new argument that sounded like all their earlier arguments. Duke volunteered to mark the spot but got voted down because he was Jim Dandy's little bird. In the end, I got nominated as the only one they all sort of trusted. Translation: I looked too scared to try anything sneaky. Letting me mark the spot satisfied everyone but Duke, who warned me not to mess up.

"Or else."

So I found myself alone on a dark sandbar, not even a torch at my side. Light might attract company, they said. When a passing barge blew its horn, I nearly jumped out of my skin. Barges had always sounded kind of sad and regal when I was comfy at home in my own bed, but out on the night river, they sounded wild and dragonish.

Time's hard to gauge when you're all alone in the dark, with the river rolling along beside you, but it felt as though Duke and the trolls were gone nearly as long as the dinosaurs have been. Eventually they returned, arguing their way over the last dune, their backs stooped beneath piles of mining equipment. Duke trudged along behind, carting more than his share. With the trolls so busy bickering about who would do the shoveling and who would do the sifting, Duke took it upon himself to play Mr. Hotshot when I made the mistake of asking a question.

"What do they need the ukulele for?" I asked.

"You've got to sing to a star," Duke informed me, "or it burns itself out."

I pointed out six oven mitts on top of the pile of mining equipment they'd dumped on the ground.

"What do you think?" Duke sneered. "Stars are hot."

There were shovels, normal store-bought ones. No need to explain those, except that an anchor was tied to each shovel handle by a thick vine.

"Anchors?"

"In case of cave-ins," Duke said.

There were catcher's masks, along with catcher's chest guards and shin guards. Also, a fishbowl.

"You'll see," Duke told me.

I saw scarfs, possibly knitted by mothers, and plastic buckets tied to vines. Stick ladders lay atop a large stack of driftwood. I was asking about a large roll of orange shag carpet when Jim Dandy drowned me out by shouting at Biz and Stump.

"All right, if you're so afraid of getting burnt, I'll do the sifting."

"Ain't afraid of nothing," Biz squeaked.

"Me either," Stump said.

But they seemed relieved just the same. Without another word, they drew a large circle in the sand and started digging inside it.

Outside the circle, they dropped the anchors tied to their shovels. Sand flew. Grit filled the air as the mineshaft bored straight down. The trolls wrapped the hand-knit scarfs around their faces to keep sand out. There weren't any scarfs left over, so Duke had to keep his mouth shut—a small blessing.

My cousin and I stood next the mineshaft, holding a screen door flat like a table between us. Jim Dandy poured bucket after bucket of sand on the screen, which worked like a sieve. Fine sand was sifted through, while larger pebbles and rocks were caught on top. Jim Dandy checked the pebbles and rocks by poking each one with his claw tip. If a stone wasn't hot, he picked it up, sniffed it once or twice, and chucked it over his shoulder.

Midnight came. Midnight went. The trolls dug on, slapping up driftwood retaining walls to stop loose sand from backfilling the hole. Working as fast as ten men, they soon needed the ladders. There were cave-ins, but the anchor ropes tied to their shovels allowed them to pull themselves out and keep right on digging.

"I can smell a sweet one," Jim Dandy finally called out.

Then I caught a whiff of something too, a scent not so much of burnt cheese as burnt caramel. Still, it was close enough to burnt cheese to make me believe that Duke actually had smelled something earlier.

Then, without warning, Jim Dandy jerked away from the screen.

"Ow!" he cried, waving his hand around. "Hot! Get the fishbowl!"

Duke panicked, dropped his end of the screen, and dove for the fishbowl. Pebbles flew everywhere.

"No-o-o-o!" Jim Dandy wailed.

Lunging for the hot stone, Jim Dandy got tangled up with the screen door, his foot punching right through it. All the commotion brought Biz and Stump racing up the ladder.

"It's here somewhere," Jim Dandy shouted. By then he'd shaken loose of the screen and was crawling on the sand, digging with his paws.

Biz and Stump scrambled around beside him. Duke pitched in too, desperate to make up for having dropped the screen door.

"It's here," Jim Dandy cried. "It burned me good."

But they found nothing.

Or at least they found nothing until I spied a yellow-red glow in the sand about twenty feet away.

"What's that?" I asked.

The spot I'd noticed was shining under the sand like an underwater light in a nighttime fountain.

"It's diving!" Biz squeaked.

All three trolls leaped after it, whipping sand between their legs like dogs would. When they caught up to the star, Jim Dandy grabbed the fishbowl and scooped it up. Biz stacked a bucket atop the bowl, trapping it.

Without a word, they jumped into their catcher's masks and chest protectors and shin guards.

Duke and I had our noses pressed as close to the fishbowl as possible, without touching it. Inside the bowl, a bumblebee-size pebble pinged off the glass, glowing like an exploding diamond. The longer it ricocheted around, the fiercer its color, turning from yellow-red to a hot, pure white. Its buzz turned shriller, like a distant fire alarm. The smell of burnt caramel grew stronger.

Once dressed in their catcher's outfits, the trolls pulled on their oven mitts and went into a crouch. From somewhere in the distance came a faint buzz that matched the louder one inside the fishbowl.

"Twelve o'clock!" Stump cried, pointing directly above them.

A swarm of stars came slamming out of the sky faster than hummingbirds, brighter than mirrors at noon, louder than a hive of sprayed bees.

Duke covered his head.

I nearly did, but it was too amazing to miss. It was like being caught inside a thundercloud full of lightning. It was like riding a fireworks rocket that had just exploded. It was like having a storm of beautiful sparks trapped behind your eyelids as you slept. They swooped down on us, aiming for the fishbowl.

The trolls waited, crouched behind their oven mitts. Two or three stars got past them, bouncing off the fishbowl. Fast and blinding as they were, they still couldn't do any damage to the glass.

"Got one!" Biz shrieked, dancing about with his oven mitts clasped together.

Stump made a desperate leap at another but missed. Jim Dandy impersonated a wooden post, maybe hoping a star would land in his mitt, maybe hoping one wouldn't.

As soon as Biz made his catch, the swarm of shooting stars lifted away as if scared. They hovered briefly overhead before flashing back into the night sky.

"Cowards!" Jim Dandy shouted, coming to life just in time to shake a fist at them.

But the stars kept right on going until they vanished in the distance, leaving the night sky as calm and peaceful as an untouched pond.

"What are they?" I asked.

"Wouldn't you like to know," Duke said, hoping to sound as if he did.

thirty one

DUKE'S LIE

With his oven mitts clasped together, Biz danced around, squealing, "A box! Get a box! This thing's hot!"

There was a clumsy scramble, with Stump digging through the driftwood and Jim Dandy checking inside buckets.

"The carpet!" Biz squeak-shouted. "We put them inside the carpet."

Stump unrolled the carpet and found three jewelry boxes wrapped inside it, one made of mirrors, one of seashells, one of dark wood with a ballerina figurine on top. Grabbing the mirror box, Stump popped its lid and held it up with his eyes closed. Biz threw his catch inside, clicked the lid shut, then grabbed the box, yelling, "The ukulele! Quick!"

The jewelry box was rattling so fiercely that Biz was shaking from head to toe.

Jim Dandy ran for the ukulele and handed it off to Stump, who took a deep breath to calm himself before he started softly strumming. At first, with Biz thumping around on the sand, you could barely hear Stump, but he kept at it in a low, surprisingly gentle voice, singing a lullaby.

The water's rippling sweetly.
The river's snoring deeply.
The fish are deftly strumming.
The willows softly humming.

And then he sang in a deep, deep voice:

Now that little trolls are in bed.

He went on:

The candle's burning real low.
The west wind is your pillow.
The snakes are all done scheming.
The lilies are all dreaming.

Now that little trolls are in bed.

The tadpoles quiet way down.
The catfish swim to Sleep Town.
The night is gently drumming.
The sand-snail soon is coming.

Now that little trolls are in bed.

The lullaby may have been for baby trolls, but it soothed shooting stars too, settling down the jewelry box in Biz's hands. The shooting star in the fishbowl quit beating around and lay at the bottom of the bowl, a pulse of light faint as a Day-Glo Band-Aid. I began to nod off myself.

The only one not slowed by the lullaby was Jim Dandy. Lifting the bucket off the fishbowl, he slid a hand over its top and whispered to Duke, "Get a jewelry box."

But Duke's eyes had been lowering with everyone else's. When

Jim Dandy repeated himself, I fought off the nods and picked up a second jewelry box, the one with the ballerina on top. As soon as I flipped the lid open, Jim Dandy turned the fishbowl upside down and shook the star into it.

"Close it!"

The instant I clicked the lid shut, I knew I'd done something terribly wrong. Inside the jewelry box, the star came to life, dinging about so fast that it made the ballerina twirl. The vibrations rattled my teeth. It was a musical jewelry box, so it played a tune too, the same lullaby that Stump had sung. Gradually the ballerina atop the box slowed to a stop, the song faded, the star went back to sleep. I set the box on the sand and stepped away from it, ashamed. By then everyone else had woken up and was wild with excitement.

"I think that's two!" Jim Dandy crowed. "Almost three!"

They went back to sniffing up stars again, faster than ever, for the night was wearing thin and dawn was on its way. Duke and I were told to fill in the first mineshaft while they searched.

"Biz is planning on turning you to stone," I warned my cousin as I shoveled.

"Oh, I'm sure," Duke sniped, in a snit because I'd helped Jim Dandy with the musical box.

"Stump says we shouldn't go anywhere near this Bo the Great Rock Troll."

"As if he'd know."

"And Jim Dandy can't wait to drop you off the wagon wheel bridge."

"I'm shaking in my booties," Duke fake gasped.

So much for troll advice.

"At least we won't have school tomorrow," I said, wanting to say something he couldn't disagree with. Tomorrow was Monday, but it didn't look like we'd be reading any books. "I suppose you'll miss the kids you pick on."

"That bunch of ninnies?"

"I bet you miss 'em," I insisted. "I even think that deep down you miss your parents too."

"No way," Duke growled. "I've never had it so good."

He got quiet after that, so I should have figured that he was scheming.

Stump's toy poodle soon started yipping at the far end of the sandbar, and Duke tore off to see what they'd found. It took me fewer than ten steps to catch up with him and two more to race past him. As I pulled even, Duke stumbled and fell flat. I kept right on going. At the time I didn't even wonder about Duke's clumsiness, but later on I thought about it plenty, for all the good it did me. I'd never known my cousin to lose his balance when trying to be first in line.

"It's faint!" Jim Dandy was shouting when I found them. His nose funnels were pressed to the ground.

They went straight to work. Since this star was closer to the river, the sand they shoveled soon turned wet and heavy. Their mood grew dark as the wire mesh of the second screen door sagged and then gave out. But on went the digging. The mesh of the third screen was sagging badly when Biz finally squeaked, "We got heat!"

Another few bucketfuls and the color came, the sand flashing purple and white and smelling more like burnt cheese than with the first.

"Whiff that," Jim Dandy said, inhaling. "Must be an old-timer."

"Fishbowl!" Stump yelled, still digging.

I started to reach for the fishbowl, but Duke tripped me and got it himself. As you might expect, his nose suffered for that stunt, but he handed the fishbowl down the ladder just in time for Stump to scoop up their third star. It pinged around inside the fishbowl more sluggishly than the first two, and they had no trouble dropping it in the seashell jewelry box. That done, they howled at a rising crescent moon that was thin as a finger-nail clipping, orange as a pumpkin headed for pie. They beat their chests like monkey men and slapped one another on the backs as if there'd never been a cross word between them.

"What'd I tell you?" Jim Dandy cheered. "What did I tell you?"

"Make way," Biz squealed haughtily. "Bow down."

"You see!" Stump shouted into the darkness, as if he'd proven himself to the universe.

Through all the celebrating, Duke stood off to the side, shuffling his feet and looking worried. When Stump unexpectedly tried to dance with him, my cousin yanked his arm free and announced, "I'm afraid I've got some bad news, boys."

His imitation of Jim Dandy's smoothness wasn't all that smooth. The trolls didn't hear him at first, so Duke had to raise his voice to a half shout.

"My cousin let one of your stars go."

The dancing stopped. The hooting died. My breathing, blinking, and thinking came to a halt with everything else.

"Am I hearing you right?" Jim Dandy said, looking kind of sick.

"I'm afraid so," Duke answered. "She would have let the other one go too, if I hadn't stopped her."

So now I knew why Duke had stumbled and fell when we'd been racing to the third star. He'd wanted his friends to be one star short so that they'd have to offer food to Bo. He planned on being the one to carry that food, and best of all—from Duke's view—he'd figured out a way to pin it all on me. All of a sudden the three trolls were making hard raspy sounds in their throats, and the green torches were making their eyes glow.

"She said she felt sorry for them," Duke told them.

"This is all your fault," Biz squeaked grimly at Jim Dandy. "You're the one wanting these two along."

"Hold on, now," Jim Dandy said, scrambling. "You boys knew we'd have some troubles along the way. All the songs said we would."

"You're not wiggling out of this one," Biz squeaked. "So what are you going to do about it?"

"Do? Why, I don't plan on doing anything, except make these two pay for our losses."

"Now, wait a minute," Duke squawked. "She's the one let the star out."

"Wasn't me," I piped up. "It was him."

Not knowing which of us to believe, they tied us both up with vines.

thirty-two

THREE BAGS & A GNOME

We spent the day at the wet bottom of a twenty-foot mineshaft. Sunlight may not turn a river troll to stone, but it does make them all cross and itchy. To block out the sun, they unrolled the orange shag carpet across the mouth of the shaft, then sprinkled sand over it for camouflage. The last troll down stuck his hand out from beneath the carpet and tossed sand over the remaining corner.

The trolls tied their alligator bags to the ladder maybe halfway down the shaft. Stump left his bag unzipped, allowing a faint green glow to seep out.

"Helps me sleep," Stump mumbled without being asked.

We lay nestled like spoons, Duke at one end of the line, me the other, our hands and feet still tied. If they could have tied my nose, I wouldn't have minded.

"So who's going to talk to Bodacious?" Biz grumble-squeaked in the greenish dark.

"I could," Duke volunteered.

Nobody paid him any mind except to laugh, but at least his offer broke the tension.

"Now, Biz," Jim Dandy reasoned, "if you talk royalty to royalty with old Bo, we should be fine. All you have to do is tell her it's a package deal. Two stars and one meal for three crickets. No, better not call it a meal, better call it a banquet. Now, that's a steal."

"Oh no," Biz protested. "You tell her. I might forget something."

"She'll take it better from an equal," Jim Dandy predicted.

Name-calling followed until Stump played peacemaker, saying, "How about a taste of those willow cats?"

That at least was something they could agree about, so they chowed down without offering us anything to eat, then dropped off to sleep, one by one. Determined to show he was one of the gang, Duke conked out with them.

They snored worse than broken trombones, but even if Jim Dandy, Biz, Stump, and Duke had been quiet sleepers, I still wouldn't have been able to nod off. Not with everything I had swirling around inside my head.

After a while, all my tossing and turning woke Stump, who was right behind me. "If I untie you," he whispered in my ear, "will you stop thrashing?"

"I'll try."

As soon as Stump undid the knots holding my wrists and ankles together, I got busy pretending to snore. In no time at all the troll's paw slipped off my shoulder and he was back to talking in his sleep. "Not me! Duckwad." I crept up the ladder, wanting a peek in the trolls' alligator bags. It seemed a likely place to stash a stone feather and glove.

Inside Stump's bag there wasn't much of anything but his toy poodle (asleep in his cage), a sack of doggie treats, and a snapshot of a chunky troll wearing a stick hat with a water lily on top. His wife, I assumed. There was also a family picture that showed Stump, a motherly troll in a patched apron, and another troll who must have been the missing brother, the one turned into a human. I studied the brother's face a minute, unable to shake the notion that I'd seen him somewhere before. How that could be, I had no idea. He was an ugly brute, with a leech sucking the tip of his snout, flies hovering above his ears, and riverweed stuck between his teeth. Still, there was something about his eyes . . .

And that's when it hit me: Duckwad's eyes gazed into the camera the same way my eyes looked into the bathroom mirror whenever I was studying myself. Exactly! It seemed as though he was looking for someone he'd lost. In shock, I sort of forgot to breathe for a minute or two, and, growing dizzy, I nearly fell off the ladder. This could explain some things, such as why my best friends weren't my sisters but turtles, toads, and beetles. The thought that I might be Stump's missing brother circled around inside my head without actually landing but making a lot of noise. To scare the thought away, I moved on to the next bag, feeling numb and shaky.

The green glow inside Jim Dandy's bag showed me a bottle of Ruby Gnatbreath's Amazing Mouthwash (reuseable); a tube of Delaware Wingdam's Slick-Back Hair Wax; Tutu Mudnose's Underarm Defoliant; a folding chair that said DIRECTOR on its back; a grumpy mole; and several copies of *Hollywood Glamour,* the magazine read by the stars. No stone feather or glove.

On to Biz's bag, which had a funny hum coming from inside. Putting an ear to it, I heard faint singing that stopped as soon as I touched the zipper. When I opened the bag, I found a gnome guarding its contents.

He was barely larger than my hand and held a pitchfork the size of a fork, though sharper. I could tell he was a gnome by his pointed hat and full-length beard. Moonglasses protected him from the green glow filling the bag.

"Hark," the gnome said in a small, fierce voice, "who goes there?"

"A friend of Biz's," I whispered back, saying the first thing that popped into my mouth.

"Did Mr. High-and-Mighty send my wages?" the gnome demanded.

"I'm afraid not," I said with a small yelp. Biz's crown-ring had given my middle finger a little nip. "He sent me after the stone feather."

"Now, isn't that just like him?" the gnome griped.

"How so?"

"He took that feather out of here and never brought it back, that's how so. He's just like every other Mossbottom I've done business with. Too important to keep track of the little things. Leave that to the hired help. I've half a mind to quit on him. Now clear out of here afore I make jelly out of you. You're letting all my stale air out."

And he jabbed at me with his pitchfork. He'd have drawn blood if I hadn't been quick. Zipping the bag shut from the inside, he went back to singing. This time I caught some of the words, which were mad and spiteful:

> Yes, your majesty.
> No, your majesty.
> I'd rather be home in my hole,
> Your majesty.

His voice cut off as the zipper closed.

Feeling bluer than mud, I slunk back to the bottom of the mineshaft, wondering if Mom and Dad and Grandpa and even my sisters were really my family. Even if they weren't, I felt a homesick ache just thinking of them. If I hadn't been so bothered by my resemblance to Stump's brother, I probably would have cried myself to sleep. Instead, I just cried myself awake.

thirty three

THE VALLEY

A long time later the trolls woke up and started grumbling about how they hadn't gotten any sleep. Actually, they'd stirred as much as fallen timbers the entire day and just sounded scared about their meeting with Bodacious Deepthink, the Great Rock Troll. But eventually they shifted from fretting about Bo to describing what they'd do after getting their lucky crickets, finding their fathers, and coming home heroes.

"Going to visit the Nile," Jim Dandy bragged. "I hear it's quite a river."

"Order a clamshell throne," Biz said.

"Find my brother," Stump vowed, tying up my wrists and ankles before anyone noticed I'd been loose, "and get back my collection of fish scales."

Hearing that didn't leave me feeling too proud—if I was his brother, I mean. At least all the talk made the trolls braver. Pretty soon, they sent Stump up the ladder for a peek outside.

"It's dark," he called down.

We were off. Except for one piece of driftwood, they stashed all their mining equipment in the mineshaft, which they covered up with carpet. The piece of driftwood they dragged along was a stout pole about twice my height. After tying me to the pole, Biz and Stump lifted it to their shoulders, which put me between them, hanging upside down.

"I can walk," I offered.

"No, you can't," Biz squeaked.

"When you see old Bo," Jim Dandy chuckled, "you might decide to run."

"What about Duke?" I was watching Jim Dandy untie my cousin's feet and hands. "You're letting him walk."

"We need him to carry Bo's meal," Jim Dandy said.

"You mean banquet," Duke corrected, shouldering a heavy burlap sack that Jim Dandy had pulled out of the mining supplies.

"That's right," Jim Dandy said, clapping my cousin on the back. "Banquet."

Duke groaned beneath the bag of mutton and wheels of goat cheese, its weight explaining why they wanted him to haul it. Jim Dandy even claimed he would have helped with the bag if he hadn't been wearing oven mitts and balancing the two jewelry boxes still holding stars.

Quiet as cats, we left the sandbar, crossed a marsh, and sloshed through a culvert that cut under the Wisconsin highway. A couple of miles above Big Rock, we stopped at the mouth of a long, twisty valley that led away from the river.

"Remember," Biz cautioned, "we don't answer any of her riddles."

Woods covered the valley's hillsides; pastures and a creek filled its middle. We stayed in the woods on an old Indian trail, or maybe it was an old troll trail. Our progress went like this: two steps and a stop, two steps and a listen. Nobody talked, except to say "Shhh."

Even Duke buttoned his lip.

As the valley narrowed, we slipped by farms where watchdogs

slept and hollow trees where owls blinked. The trolls' slow march meant it took most of the night to move up the valley, with me hanging upside down all the way.

At last we ran smack into a limestone wall and had to stop. Biz and Stump dumped me in a small grassy clearing before the wall, which climbed straight up for twenty or thirty feet.

We sat before the rock wall for the rest of the night, which lasted most of a century. When the pearly gray of false dawn finally arrived, a new moon came fleeing before it, rising up out of the earth as if chased by rock trolls. Or so it seemed. All I could see of the new moon was a faint silvery outline, a silhouette of a full moon, but with it came what everything in the valley had been waiting for.

At first I wasn't sure what it was. A sound? A touch? A shadow moving fast? I knew only that for a beat everything, everywhere, stopped. The trolls locked up in midbreath. The stars lost their twinkle. The new moon got stuck. The valley waited.

Then I realized it was a sound. A single trembly note cut through the woods like a mosquito buzzing through tall grass. The note lingered for nearly a minute, making everything shivery, and then it was gone. On its heels, a rustle swept through the valley as everything scrambled for a better hiding place. That was followed by a stillness that made you hold your breath longer than you thought possible.

"What was that?" Duke asked, not sounding as if he really wanted to know.

"Bodacious Deepthink." Stump gulped.

"She's waiting," Biz squeaked.

"Boys," Jim Dandy quaked, "so are those crickets."

A new, colder note cut through the woods now, and there could be no doubt: it came from the rock wall before us. If my hands had been free, I would have covered my ears. Duke did cover his ears.

The note didn't bother Jim Dandy, Biz, or Stump, though. In fact, it seemed to make up their minds for them. Or at least it made up Biz's mind.

"Enough talk," Biz squeaked, his voice so high that it disappeared at the end.

Stepping up to the rock wall, he knocked on it the way you might knock on the door of a dark castle.

Getting no answer, he knocked louder.

That was when the earth started to shake. Stone scraped. In the middle of the rock face, a dark hole slowly opened from the ground up. Inside the cave, a lantern was coming toward us.

—thirty-four—
BODACIOUS DEEPTHINK

A mountaintop must have once fallen on Bodacious Deepthink. She looked squashed enough. She also looked as though she were turning into stone. All the while she hobbled toward us, she grinned crookedly as a rockslide.

Supported by a wooden staff, she had three or four times the girth of a river troll, though was no taller than one. She had bulgy eyes that clicked whenever she blinked, ears like tree fungus, and hair that sparkled like orange crystals. Only her snout vaguely resembled the river trolls', though without whiskers. Her fingers were like petrified tree roots; her toes, thicker petrified tree roots. She wore a nylon bicyclist's outfit that was tiger-striped and bulged like a parachute filled with gravestones. Her earrings were live bats, the kind with wings.

"You boys are running late," she grumbled, holding up her lantern for a better view of us.

About that lantern: it was made of brass and glass and had a shooting star rolling around inside it. Whenever the star dimmed, Bodacious Deepthink revived it by rapping the top of the lantern with a stone key that made the same shivery note that had knifed through the valley.

"Any of you boys belong to Two-cents Eel-tongue's brood?" Bodacious Deepthink asked.

Hearing that, Jim Dandy fainted. Keeled right over.

"I'll take that as a yes." Bodacious Deepthink snickered. "Anybody else feeling weak?"

Biz was too tongue-tied to squeak, although to his credit he at least opened his mouth. Stump covered his eyes with his hands, the way a two-year-old will when trying to hide. The only river troll with enough wits to answer wasn't a full-fledged river troll at all but my cousin Duke. For the first time in my life, I felt kind of proud of the rat.

"Hey," Duke spoke out, brassy as ever. "We've come a long way to see you."

Bodacious Deepthink held her lantern toward Duke for closer inspection.

"And who might you be?" she asked, amused by such freshness.

"Their assistant," Duke said.

By then Stump was peeking through his fingers and one of Jim Dandy's eyes was open a slit.

"And this little morsel?" she asked, holding the lantern toward me.

"His conscience," I blurted.

"Quiet, you," Duke growled, giving the bottom of my shoes a kick. He might have given me two kicks, but as soon as his foot nicked mine, he let out a yelp and grabbed for his face as his horn shot out another inch, easy. Something strange was going on with his hands too. They seemed to be swelling.

"Well, well." Bodacious Deepthink was watching Duke's nose with interest. "Do you boys mind if I ask you a riddle?"

Nobody objected.

"Listen carefully," she instructed. Clearing her throat, she recited:

What's round when thin,
Fatter in black,
Sinks with a grin,
And never looks back?

With a smirk, she dared us to answer.

Duke checked with Jim Dandy, who quickly closed his eye, although not before giving his head a small shake no and peeking at Stump, who shook his head no and glanced at Biz, who shook his head no without taking his eyes off Duke, who for the moment had become their leader. For once Duke did as told and just stood there looking dumb. Everyone else kept close-mouthed too, which for me was an awful strain. You see, the answer popped into my head the instant I heard the riddle, almost as if I'd heard it before.

The moon.

Where I could have heard such a riddle led me around to thinking of Stump's brother again. Duckwad might have known the answer too, though just like Jim Dandy, Biz, and Stump, he most likely would have been too scared to say it. That's when I noticed another way I was like a river troll—at the moment I was too shaky to speak up myself.

"Come on," Bodacious Deepthink prodded, disgusted with our thickness. "It's a simple one."

Everybody looked at everybody again.

"We give up," Duke said at last.

"The moon," Bodacious Deepthink answered, and with that she slapped her knee, threw back her head, and laughed so hard that one of her bat earrings fell off and had to flutter back in place.

Nobody was laughing on our side, though, or maybe I would have sprung the riddle Two-cents Eel-tongue had given me. Still, I was tempted. For one thing, it was a way to prove to myself that I

wasn't terrified. But Two-cents had said it would only buy me a little time, and trussed up as I was, what good would a little time do?
So I bit my tongue and waited.

By then Jim Dandy had come around enough to sneak behind
Biz and Stump, and Biz and Stump had taken a step behind Duke.

"Boys," Bodacious Deepthink confided, "there's nothing like a
riddle to break the ice. People come up here expecting to be dinner,
but I had to give up eating the guests years ago. Heartburn. I'm on a
special diet now."

"We know." Duke lifted up the sack of food he'd been carrying.

"You can't keep a secret in this valley," Bodacious Deepthink
complained. "Do you boys mind if I ask another question? A serious
one. Hear me out." Setting her lantern down and resting both stony
hands on her staff, the Great Rock Troll closed her eyes to collect
her thoughts. Keeping her eyes shut, she went on in a surprisingly
soothing voice, "Have you ever wondered if there might be more to
life than tipping canoes or snapping fish lines? Something more sat-
isfying, I mean."

"Why, yes," Stump said, sounding as though she'd read his mind.
He lowered his hands from his face in amazement.

"And have you ever wondered where you might find that something extra?" she coaxed. "That something that might add extra satisfaction to your life?"

"I thought we were here for crickets," Duke said.

"Has anyone ever talked to you about the glories of rock?"
Bodacious Deepthink asked, a sweet smile sliding across her bumpy
face.

"Why, no," Biz squeaked, speaking up for the first time. His voice
was nowhere near as high as I would have expected.

"There's no greater peace in the world than living underground
with good rock." Bodacious Deepthink sighed contentedly. "Always

cool and dank. Everything smells moldy and wonderful. Sounds echo beautifully. Uncover a lantern—sparkles everywhere. Cover it up and you'll never see a dark as lovely and black and comforting. You can give your eyes a good long rest anytime you want when you're down below. Now doesn't that sound grand?"

Here Bodacious Deepthink popped open one eye to see how she was doing. The river trolls were spellbound, nodding their heads like a line of marionettes, although her voice wasn't working on my cousin. He was wrinkling his nose as though smelling something rotten.

"What about earthquakes?" Duke quizzed her.

"Only in nursery rhymes," she answered, closing her eye. "You've a mind full of questions? All and good. There's always room down below for a fellow with a head on his shoulders, especially if he's a horn to go with it."

To that Jim Dandy chuckled until Bodacious Deepthink silenced him by turning his way. She didn't even have to open her eyes.

"Remember," the Great Rock Troll went on in a wise voice, "I dealt with your fathers, so I know what young river trolls are after. You've come up here hoping for the crickets who can tell you what happened to those first three miners. Am I right?"

"Pretty much," Stump confessed.

"Well," she sympathized, "take my word for it, the crickets you're after don't remember a thing about those miners. Your fathers found that out the hard way."

"B-but what happened to our Dads?" Stump asked.

All three river trolls nodded eagerly at that question. When Bodacious Deepthink snapped open her eyes, she found Jim Dandy, Biz, and Stump all acting like bobbleheads. She smiled in satisfaction.

"Who knows?" she went on. "Maybe some pirates shanghaied them. I can only tell you that any father who traded for a cricket didn't know what he was getting into. Listen now"—and here she raised a hand as if taking a solemn oath—"there's nothing lucky about those three crickets. They're just common, ordinary cave crickets, and I haven't talked to a cave cricket yet whose head wasn't full of stuff and nonsense. Stories about gold and adventures are all they're good for. They keep coming back here broke and claiming they don't remember a thing about what's happened to your fathers or those three miners."

Dropping her hand, she turned deeply concerned, saying, "I can save you boys a whole world of heartache and misery, if only you'll listen. Come with me now and you'll learn the splendor of rock. You'll see sights that will take your breath away. I'll even write everything up in a contract, I will. Satisfaction guaranteed or your old life back. How's that?"

"A contract?" Biz squeaked, intrigued.

One look at Jim Dandy's dreamy smile told me he was being swayed too. Bodacious Deepthink's voice was as warm and comfy as an electric blanket on a chill night. But I still needed a stone feather.

"What exactly would they be doing?" I asked, aiming to sound as innocent and sincere as possible. "Down below, I mean."

thirty five

DOUBLE·KNOT EEL·TONGUE

It's amazing how one little question can blow up everything. Biz shuddered as if surfacing from a confusing dream. Jim Dandy turned off his smile. Stump re-covered his eyes.

"They'd be doing important work," Bo huffed, insulted. "Exciting work."

"Have you got the crickets or not?" Duke demanded.

Bodacious Deepthink blinked at Duke three times before slamming her staff down hard enough to crack a sizable rock in two. Over her shoulder she shouted toward the cave, "Double-knot Eel-tongue! Drag your worthless bones out here and have a talk with your good-for-nothing son."

A tiny piffle of air could have bowled me over. As for Jim Dandy, he looked as though someone had busted a canoe paddle over his head.

"Am I going to get to meet your dad?" Duke gushed, hardly able to believe his luck.

Jim Dandy shut him up by giving his horn a hard twist.

From inside the cave came the rattle of rickety wheels on stone. Out of the shadows trudged a bent-over river troll who dragged one foot and hummed off-key. Dented and dinged as he was, a rockslide or two must have caught him. His willow hair had mostly been stripped clean of leaves, and his scales had lost their mossy green shine and turned a dirty brown. Freckles? They'd all popped into warts.

Jim Dandy's father was pulling a kid's red wagon, which carried a bamboo birdcage. Inside the cage, three lucky crickets were clinging to the leaves of a potted plant, an ivy of some kind. They were cave crickets, the same kind as the old lady had seen in my eyes when I'd first met her.

"Park that wagon," Bodacious Deepthink fumed, "and come talk to these boys."

He parked, he came. Full daylight had a good chance of reaching us first, bad as Double-knot Eel-tongue's crooked foot dragged.

"Tell 'em how good you've got it," Bodacious Deepthink ordered, nudging him forward with her staff. "Go on. Tell 'em how they'll never get another chance so golden as this one."

From up close you could see that one of Double-knot's eyes was swollen shut and one of his ears bitten half off. He wore a tattered blue scarf around his throat. His ragged jeans were held up by a piece of yellow rope that looked as though it was cut off a motorboat's anchor line.

"Speak up," Bodacious Deepthink said, poking him again with her staff.

"Mining's the best thing ever happened to me," Double-knot Eel-tongue recited in a flat, lifeless voice. "I never knew there were such opportunities to be had underground. A real chance to contribute to the greatest undertaking known to modern trolls."

"Tell them about the moon," Bodacious Deepthink coached in a whisper.

"The moon's waiting for us," Double-knot said. "We're making great progress every day. We've the best miners in the world.

They've the finest picks and shovels. Dynamite is available. You can't imagine how good it feels to blow a rock bed to smithereens, or to find new caverns never seen before, or to scratch your back on a stalactite that's older than your grandmother."

"And every morning?" Bodacious Deepthink prompted. "When you're done working?"

"Every morning you go to bed knowing you've made a real contribution. Your work is especially valued too, because you're river trolls, you see."

"Why's that?" Stump asked, sounding impressed.

Bodacious Deepthink stepped in with an answer for him.

"On account of that cheap little curse your mothers threw on me," she chided. "We rock trolls won't find our way to the moon till those three miners find their way home. That's the way they said it. Rockfudge! Can I help it if a river troll can get lost in his own bed? Can I help it if they don't know how to handle a lucky cricket? Can I help it if . . ."

She ticked off a half-dozen other things she couldn't help, and every one of those things made her so touchy and grouchy that her bat earrings were fluttering most of the time now. But finally she managed to get a grip on herself and slow her tongue enough to talk more civilly.

"Let's just say you river trolls have got me over a barrel. Thanks to that curse, all us rock trolls are able to do is dig around and around in circles without getting anywhere. That's why we need your help. The curse can't touch you river trolls. So if you put your mind to it, you can tell us where to tunnel. It's the only way we'll ever make it to the moon. Old Double-knot here, he's been mapping our diggings for years and years, but he's lost his oomph, can't quite get us there. Don't get me wrong, he's done wonders, gotten us so close that some nights we can hear the moon humming. If we put our ears to rock, we surely can. All we need is some fresh blood, a younger river troll whose eyes and ears are sharper. Whoever takes over would be my chief engineer. Paid accordingly. A golden opportunity, especially to show your mothers who's boss. Wouldn't you agree, Double-knot?"

"Oh, yes," Double-knot croaked, his eyes glued to her staff, in case he had to dodge it.

"So what do you boys say?" Bodacious Deepthink cajoled. "It'd only take one of you. The other two can try their luck with crickets, if that's what curls their tails."

No volunteers stepped forward, so at least Jim Dandy, Biz, and Stump weren't as dumb as they currently looked.

"Tell them about the grub," Bodacious Deepthink said to Jim Dandy's father.

"Best going," Double-knot promised, though his belly didn't have any jiggle to it.

"And the accommodations?" Bodacious Deepthink added.

"Four-star."

"Your fellow workers?"

"Princes, every last one."

It was clear that Double-knot had been schooled with a hard stick.

"What about sweets?" Duke asked.

"Any time you crave them," Bodacious Deepthink said.

"Chances to bully?"

"Every day," she promised. "Helps keep up morale. Anything else?"

There wasn't, except from Duke, and Bodacious Deepthink put a stop to that by jabbing her staff hard into his gut. While my cousin was doubled over, the Great Rock Troll went on, friendly as ever, "So there you have it, boys. What do you say? I'm offering you the chance of a lifetime. Fame and glory wait for the river troll who can get us to the moon. Surely at least one of you can see that?"

When Jim Dandy, Biz, and Stump all held their ground, refusing to bite, Bodacious Deepthink's patience sprang a leak.

"The dumbest-looking one must be your son," she said to Double-knot. "Have a word with him."

Jim Dandy and his father stood there gazing into each other's eyes as if on opposite banks of the river, and a wide spot in the river at that. Double-knot made the first move by stepping forward and putting an old broken paw on Jim Dandy's shoulder.

"I swear that everything you've heard here . . ." he began.

Jim Dandy knocked the paw off his shoulder and turned his head away. Bodacious Deepthink slammed her staff down and roared, "This is your father, boy."

That's when Jim Dandy went up about a hundred notches in my estimation. Looking directly into Bodacious Deepthink's flashing eyes, he said, "No, he's not. My father came up here, got a cricket from you, went looking for those miners, and hasn't been seen since."

It was a bold-faced lie, of course. Everyone could see that. Even busted up and covered with rock dust, Double-knot looked like Jim Dandy, all the way down to the neck scarves they both wore. But the point was, Jim Dandy refused to think badly of his father.

"Tell that young fool that he's making a big mistake!" Bodacious Deepthink thundered.

That turned out to be the wrong thing to say. No, calling Jim Dandy a fool for refusing to believe the worst of his father, that set the stage for something none of us was expecting. Reaching out for Jim Dandy's shoulders, Double-knot said, "This may be my only chance to be your father, boy, so you better listen. I've some advice to share."

thirty-six

THE BANQUET

Everybody leaned forward to catch what Jim Dandy's father had to say. Straightening his bent shoulders as much as he could, Double-knot took a breath and advised, "Don't make the same mistake I did, son. Go out and make your own."

With that, he let go of Jim Dandy's shoulders and slouched back toward the cave. If there was a throat thereabouts that didn't hide a sizable lump, it wasn't mine, not after all the times I'd refused advice from my own mom and dad. Of course, Bodacious Deepthink was all cinders and gas.

Finally Jim Dandy broke the silence, saying to Bodacious Deepthink, "If you're done with the sales pitch, we came to trade for some crickets."

Hearing that, Jim Dandy's father held his head higher and picked up his pace. Bodacious Deepthink responded by whamming her staff down and shaking the entire valley.

"What have you got to trade?" she snarled.

"Two shooting stars and one meal," Biz squeaked after Jim Dandy elbowed him.

"One banquet," Jim Dandy corrected.

"That?" Bodacious Deepthink groused with a snort of disbelief.

She was pointing at Duke, who was holding up the burlap sack he'd been carrying.

"Guaranteed delicious," Duke promised.

To prove his point, he untied the neck of the sack and dumped out the food inside. Stones fell to the ground, barely missing his toes.

"Doesn't look like much." Bodacious Deepthink wrinkled her nostrils.

"He just got the horn," Jim Dandy said. "The rest is coming."

When the Great Rock Troll took two steps forward and turned Duke to the side for a better view, my cousin didn't even squawk. He was still gazing down at the stones as if expecting them to turn into goat cheese and pigs' feet and ox tails.

"Done!" Bodacious Deepthink said, liking Duke's profile. Over her shoulder, she shouted, "Bring me those crickets!"

Double-knot surprised everyone by shouting from the mouth of the cave, "Get them yourself!"

Bodacious Deepthink grumbled over to the wagon, which she shoved forward with her staff.

"These are the ones you want," Bodacious Deepthink scoffed. "Your fathers did too, except for Double-knot, of course."

The three white crickets inside the cage looked old and rickety enough to have met a lot of fathers. One had a bent antenna. Another stood lopsided. The last was drooling.

"We'll take 'em," Jim Dandy said, reaching.

"Stars first." Bo batted Jim Dandy's hands away with her staff.

When Jim Dandy handed over the jewelry boxes, Bodacious Deepthink sniffed them without opening the lids.

"They'll do." She wasn't impressed.

"Say," Duke bawled, finally coming to his senses, "what happened to the mutton and goat cheese and stuff?"

Duke looked from Jim Dandy to Biz to Stump, all of whom were too busy admiring crickets to answer.

"You're with me," Bodacious Deepthink said to my cousin. "Come on."

"Run!" I shouted.

But he didn't. All he managed to do was stare—in disbelief—as Bodacious Deepthink lifted a rope from the wagon and lassoed him so expertly that you knew she'd done it before. Reeling Duke in, the Great Rock Troll tucked him over her shoulder and turned toward the cave.

"What's going on?" Duke cried out.

"Take your crickets," Bodacious Deepthink bellowed above Duke's wails. "Leave the cage."

With that, the Great Rock Troll plodded toward the cave as if she couldn't even feel Duke thrashing about.

Spotting me on the ground, Duke pointed and screamed, "Take her! Take Claire! She'll do whatever . . ."

He never got around to finishing his offer. Right then he let out such an ear-splitting yowl that Jim Dandy, Biz, and Stump all stopped admiring crickets and straightened up as if something house-size had exploded. Duke's horn shot out another six inches. His arms thickened, legs too. The seams on his black zipper coat ripped everywhere as his skin puckered with wrinkles. Unfurling like leaves opening in spring, his ears shot upward with fur tufts on top. He turned black-gray, everywhere, and his fingers melded together into hooves.

A tail split his pants.

"That's more like it," Bodacious Deepthink said, happy at last.

She didn't flinch under the added weight but barked to Double-knot, "Get the wagon!"

This time Jim Dandy's father obeyed, although not before saying,

"Just remember one thing, son: these crickets are the worst kind of liars. Every last one of them."

With that, he opened the cage door, scooped out the three decrepit crickets, and placed one on the shoulder of each river troll. Jim Dandy got his last.

"W-why don't you come with us," Jim Dandy sputtered.

"Don't think it's not tempting," Double-knot whispered, "but I've made my choices. And who knows? I might do something good here yet." Picking up the wagon handle, he started toward the cave, calling over his shoulder, "You boys better get moving. Bo's been known to change her mind."

About then I heard one last blubbering wail from just inside the cave.

"Take her, not me!"

Duke remained tucked over Bodacious Deepthink's stony shoulder, still pointing a hoof at me.

thirty-seven

A HERO, A HERO, A HERO

Duke's cries dwindled until the cave swallowed them completely. For a bit longer I heard the creaking wagon that Double-knot was pulling. After that, the glow from Bodacious Deepthink's lantern swayed back and forth until suddenly winking out. From inside the earth came a pop and crinkle as the cave door began to slide down. Just as morning's sunlight first nicked the treetops, the cave's mouth was gone. Solid rock faced us again.

"We did it," Stump whispered, hardly daring to believe it.

For once only Jim Dandy had nothing to say. He stood there staring at where his father had been. The cricket perched on his shoulder said, "Take your time. I'm sure she won't be back."

"You know what that means," Biz squeaked, trying to shove his way past the others.

"What about Duke?" I called out, still tied to the pole and lying on the ground.

But they weren't in any mood for listening, only running, although my voice did slow Biz enough to bend over and slip his crown-ring off my finger.

"Mine," he squeaked before dashing after the others.

So much for a troll's pledge.

"Where's the fire?" Biz's cricket cried out, which made the river trolls sprint all the faster.

"What about me?" I shouted.

That only spurred them all the more. Moving on all fours with their tails between their legs, they plowed through thickets, clawed over each other to gain the lead, never looked back.

"Hey!" I screamed.

The words echoed around the clearing. There was only one set of ears available to hear them, and that set belonged to me. By then the three river trolls were nothing but snapping branches and squeals farther down the valley.

I tried standing, fell. I tried chewing through the leather straps binding me, gagged. Whatever type of beast the leather was cut from, it burned in my mouth. Every other second I glanced toward the rock wall, praying it stayed closed. My only other option seemed to be crying. I'd just started making a puddle when someone came crashing back into the clearing.

Blundering to my rescue was Stump. The look of terror that twisted his snout said he'd come back against his better judgment. At least the cricket riding his shoulder had the decency to urge him forward by singing out, "You're a hero, a hero, a hero."

"Shut up, you," Stump hissed.

At first I thought he was warning me, but when the cricket wouldn't quit with the hero stuff, Stump grabbed him, stuffed him into a vest pocket of his bicycling togs, and zipped the pocket shut. From another pocket he whipped out a knife made from horn and began cutting my straps.

"Liars," he muttered.

"Who?" I said, so relieved at being rescued that I didn't have enough sense to keep my mouth closed and let him concentrate on freeing me.

"Cave crickets," he said. "Legend has it that one of them promised to lead Bo to the moon, and when it didn't happen, she dropped a curse on them, turned them all into liars. Come on."

By then he'd sliced through the leather strips and was pulling me to my feet. He started back down the valley without seeing if I followed. What else would I be doing?

Once the circulation to my hands and feet returned, I soon caught up with Stump. A few hundred yards later we both met up with Jim Dandy and Biz, who were leaning against trees, trying to catch their wind. As soon as we reached them, they sprinted off again, leaving us behind. Between gasps, I told Stump, "Thanks."

"Your shouting," he said, pausing to suck down a breath, "reminded me of Duckwad."

thirty eight

A BLUE-WING FAIRY

The pounding of our footsteps slowly woke the valley. Across the way a farm dog yipped, and high above a flock of geese honked. Over and over the crickets lied about being bold and brave and ten feet tall. Since they didn't sing in unison, it sounded as though a dozen of them were traveling with us.

Biz led the way, charging ahead as if chased by hellhounds, a trail of snapped branches and flattened bushes in his wake. We didn't brake until back to the sandbar, where we heard a ukulele being played. That brought everyone to a screeching halt right at the lip of the mineshaft we'd been hurrying toward. Inside the mine the strumming continued.

Circling, the trolls sniffed and muttered and whimpered as the crickets fell silent. I put my nose to work too but whiffed only river muck.

Along with the ukulele came snatches of singing. High and sweet, the voice had the river trolls covering their ears and on the verge of bolting, but before they could take off the music stopped. Everyone played statue. The carpet cover-ing the mineshaft got poked up and out peeked a pair of shiny eyes that made the crickets shift uneasily on the trolls' shoulders.

"About time," a peevish voice said from the mine.

Never had a reprimand been more welcome — at least by me. The voice belonged to the old lady.

"You?" Biz squeaked.

"And look what I found," she quipped, holding up a blue ukulele. Her moment of triumph didn't last long as she noticed someone was missing from our group and crossly said, "Where's the one with the horn?"

That had the trolls shuffling.

"Bo got him," I told her.

"That wasn't our fault," Jim Dandy protested.

"Oh, I'm sure," the old lady scolded as she climbed out of the mine.

"You've got to understand," Jim Dandy pleaded. "We had our three stars until these humans let one go. What choice did that leave us?"

The old lady sized up Jim Dandy as if he were a blister. He fiddled with his neck scarf and squirmed accordingly.

"I'm glad you brought up choices," the old lady said at last, "because you've got two things that need doing, and I'm going to let you choose which goes first. Ears working?"

"Yes, ma'am," the trolls mumbled.

Pointing the ukulele at them, the old lady ditched all her sweetness, replacing it with fire and ice.

"Choice one — you visit some people you recently turned to stone and change them back."

"We were headed that way," Jim Dandy sang out.

The old lady cut him off. "Save it. Choice two — you pay Bo another visit and rescue the kid with the horn."

"What about our fathers?" Biz squeaked-whined.

"They'll keep."

"Tackle Bo," the crickets counseled.

Hearing that advice settled it. They quickly agreed on ignoring the cricket's lies, for nobody was eager to parade back up the valley we'd just trampled down. Lining up behind the old lady, the trolls shuffled toward the river like prisoners in chains. The old lady and I were the only ones stepping lively. At the water's edge, Jim Dandy bypassed the old lady's rowboat, heading for his dugout canoe, but the old lady put a stop to that by announcing:

"You'll all be riding with me, Jim Dandy Eel-tongue, where I can keep an eye on you. And if there's any funny business, I'll turn you all into books. Thick ones with no pictures and tiny print."

Fast as they jumped aboard her boat, they must have been as terrified of reading as they were of counting. The old lady lagged behind as if they'd forgotten something.

"So where's the stone feather you used?" she asked, crossing her arms.

"Duke's house," Biz squeaked.

"It better be," she threatened, wading to the back of her boat without bothering to lift her skirt. "Here, put these on."

Pulling three floppy straw hats from a wooden chest, she held them out to the trolls.

"What's that?" Stump shied away from the hat brim facing him. It was covered with roses and bluebells that smelled freshly picked and made his snout twitch as if peppered.

"Disguises," the old lady answered. "I don't want any fisher-men spotting you. Might slow us down."

Gulping a deep breath, Stump accepted the hat and tried tugging it on. Jim Dandy and Biz followed suit. They were all trembling so hard they missed their heads by a mile.

"Claire," the old lady said, climbing aboard and waving for me to follow, "would you mind giving them a hand? I've got to arrange a ride for us in Blue Wing."

Digging a scrap of paper out of her apron pocket, the old lady got busy scribbling. Tugging off a wet sneaker, she stuffed her note inside it and flung the shoe into the river. A muskrat nabbed the shoe at once, diving out of sight.

By then I'd started tugging straw hats onto the trolls. Tying the strings under their scaly chins was the trickiest part. Every time I tried, they pulled away as if I were planning to strangle them. Whenever I leaned closer, the crickets riding their shoulders would whisper, "She's not a blue-wing fairy."

"Oh, yes she is," Stump said miserably.

thirty-nine

THE OLD LADY'S OLDER BROTHER

She may not have had lacy wings or been small enough to hide under a teacup, but the old lady handled the boat as easily as a fairy steering a leaf. Even without a motor, sail, or paddle, we flew down the river. To change the boat's direction, she simply pointed where she wanted to go. When she wanted the boat to slow down or speed up, she twisted a silver ring on her left hand as if it was a throttle. The trolls kept an awfully close eye on that silver ring, turning jumpy whenever she touched it.

"Ah, are you really a blue-wing?" I stuttered.

"Your great-great-great-grandfather once asked me the same question," she said, amused.

"Are we talking about Huntington Bridgewater?" I asked in the name of accuracy.

"We are."

"What'd you tell him?" I didn't even bother to bring up how she could be old enough to have known him.

"That it sounded to me like he'd been talking to river trolls."

She blocked more questions by picking up her ukulele and serenading the river trolls, who plugged their ears and held their breath beneath the flowery hats. They looked like three plums about to explode.

And so the ride downriver went. Fishermen in high-powered boats skipped past us, tipping their hats to all the old ladies they thought they saw in our boat. Barges going upriver rocked us with their wake.

We pulled into a landing above Blue Wing, where a well-polished white van awaited us. The door of the van said in gold letters:

COINS, GEMS, RUNESTONES,
RIDDLES & OTHER IMPONDERABLES
WING REPAIR ON OCCASION

The same letters had been on the coin shop door where the sheriff had stopped for silver dollars.

The man standing beside the van held a wet orange sneaker. His sharply pressed bib overalls and billed cap with corn logo made him look like a retired dairy farmer, but the old lady introduced him as her older brother. It fit, I guess. They both had finely spun white hair, were tall, and wore orange tennis shoes, which the old man hadn't bothered to lace. He wasn't what you'd call friendly, more what you'd call prickly.

"You trolls get in the back of the van," he ordered, "where you can't be seen. We don't want to throw the townspeople into a dither."

"Do we have keep wearing these?" Biz complained, pointing to the hat atop his head.

"Not in my van you don't."

Sailing their hats at the old lady, the trolls piled in back as if afraid the hats would follow them. I sat up front with the old lady, the old man, and a white-faced golden retriever named Pumpkin. Hearing that Pumpkin was some kind of royalty wouldn't have surprised me. She held herself regally and didn't bother to sniff me even once.

From the back of the van came singsong voices of complaint.

"Crickets," the old man grumbled before starting the motor. "Where to?"

"You'll have to ask my associate," the old lady told him.

Having never been anyone's associate before, it took me a bit to catch on, but when I saw them both looking at me, I figured it out.

"The No Leash Dog Obedience College," I directed.

The way Pumpkin barked her approval, I guessed she'd been there before and made friends with Uncle Norm. Even the old man lightened up a bit, his mood upgrading from prickly to just crusty.

"So what'd you step into this time?" he asked his sister.

"I'm trying to help my associate here bring her grandfather back to life."

"Stone?" he asked.

"Solid. The trolls in back claim to have the feather."

"You don't know?"

"Haven't seen it yet."

"Those are river trolls," the old man pointed out, "in case you haven't noticed. You may never see it. That one in back who's acting too proud to be here — he belong to the Mossbottoms?"

"He does."

"Suppose he thinks he's a king."

"The idea's occurred to him," the old lady admitted.

"Doesn't it always," the old man muttered. "Suppose the short one's a Fishfly, trying to prove something."

"I'd say he's already proved it," the old lady said, sticking up for Stump. "They've been up to Bo's, you know."

"The smarmy one an Eel-tongue?"

"Naturally."

The old man harrumphed and nodded toward me. "This one here a Bridgewater?"

"How'd you know that?" I asked.

"You've got the look," he said. A second later he confessed, "That, and Sheriff Pope's been by three times to see if I've heard anything about you."

"Was my mom or dad with him?" I asked.

"Your dad," he said. "Didn't look like he'd been getting much sleep."

forty

MORE STONE (AGAIN)

Since we reached Duke's house in broad daylight, the old man pulled up to the garage so that we could smuggle the trolls inside. The back door was still hanging open, the Beware of Dog sign draped on the handle, right where we'd left it, and everything in the kitchen stood exactly as before: Uncle Norm and Aunt Phyllis leaned over the breakfast table; Grandpa and the doctor and the policeman were piled around them like toppled bowling pins; Duff crouched under the table, the back of Grandpa B's head touching the tip of his tail. The old golden retriever named Pumpkin whined and pawed at the floor in front of Duff, trying to wake him.

The only addition to the scene was a sparrow who'd flown through the open door and landed atop Uncle Norm's head. It'd been turned to stone with its beak wide open.

I think I'd been secretly hoping that my mom and dad—or even a sister or deputy—would be moping around Duke's place, fussing about me. They'd take one look at Biz, Stump, and Jim Dandy and forbid me from spending another second with such company. (Adventures can become bothersome things, especially when there's nobody around to tell you to quit them.) When I saw they weren't there, I exhaled hard and tried to keep my chin up. The old lady saw through the act and handed me a scrap of paper, along with a pencil stubbin.

"Leave a note," she suggested. "Tell them you'll be all right."

"I will?"

"As long as I have anything to say about it," the old lady said, patting my shoulder.

So I wrote the note, just to keep my folks from worrying, and also to remind my sisters that feeding a fly to the toad named Three wouldn't kill them.

While I was busy scribbling, the old lady said to the trolls, "Time to do your stuff, boys."

"Look under the dog," Biz squeaked.

The haughty way he said it, you just knew that poking around under a stone dog was way beneath a future king.

"How'd it get under there?" the old lady asked.

"Accident," Jim Dandy swore as if under oath. "Somebody knocked it out of my hand."

"Accident my foot," the old man said with a snort. "Most likely the three of you were fighting over it."

"All right, all right," the old lady refereed. "So where's the stone glove?"

Biz looked one way, Jim Dandy the other, so the old lady zeroed in on Stump, who hung his head and confessed, "Broke to bits. When we fell on it."

So. They'd been lying to me all along and probably hadn't intended to lift a finger to help Grandpa and the others. I stood there feeling limp as a rag doll. Buttons would have been fine for my eyes, little as I'd been seeing. When Stump half raised a hand toward me, I turned my back to him.

"We'll need a stone to pry up the dog," the old lady observed, taking command.

"I've got just the thing in my van," her brother answered, heading for the door.

"Hold on," Biz squeaked. "I won't allow anything that might hurt that feather. It belongs to my Great-Aunt Tar. It's her pride and joy."

"We wouldn't be talking about Tar-and-feathers Slice-toe, would we?" asked the old man, stopping short of the door.

"That's no concern of yours," Biz squeaked, fidgeting.

"Oh, I wouldn't count on that," the old man drawled. "Some years back she broke into my store and walked off with my prize feather. I've been looking for it ever since."

"Impossible," Biz indignantly squeaked. "Great-Aunt Tar wouldn't be caught dead inside a store."

"Don't I wish," the old man muttered. Then louder, "And if she passed the feather on to you, then I'm putting my claim forward right now. This feather we're after rightfully belongs to me."

"Well," Biz hedged, "she didn't exactly pass it on to us."

"Stole it, huh?"

"Borrowed."

"Jim Dandy talked us into it," Stump volunteered.

"I don't care how you came by it," the old lady interrupted, having heard enough. "You could have sent away for it from a wishing catalogue, for all I care. Right now we need to get the feather out from under the dog. So I repeat: We need a stone glove."

"*My* feather," the old man warned, pointing an angry finger at Biz before heading outside to his van.

A couple of minutes later he returned with a marble arm that looked as though it'd once belonged to a Greek statue. The hand at the end of the arm had lost a pinky somewhere through the ages, but otherwise it looked none the worse for wear. The old man also brought in the stiffest glove I'd ever seen. Stone, from the looks of it.

"For the feather," he said, handing the glove over to his sister with a bow.

"At least you're good for something," she commented.

Holding up the stone arm, he said, "I'll need a fulcrum."

We dug a saucepan out of a cupboard and set it upside down near Duff. Resting the marble arm's elbow atop the pan, the old man wedged its fingers under Duff's stone bottom and pushed down on the upper end of the arm, prying Duff up.

"Careful, careful," Biz squeaked.

"Can you see it?" the old lady asked.

Stump and Jim Dandy had dropped to their hands and knees, then laid their heads sideways on the floor. I joined them.

"Not yet," I reported.

"Higher," Jim Dandy ordered, motioning upward.

"Careful, careful."

"Now?" the old lady asked.

"Can't tell," I said. "There's shadows."

"Well, look," Biz squeaked, so worked up that he'd planted a hand on Stump's back and was leaning over for a squint himself.

"We need more light," Jim Dandy called out.

"There's a flashlight out in my toolbox," the old man grunted, still pushing down on the stone arm.

The old lady sent me to fetch it, and without too much digging I found an old metal one that had an orange sticker on its bottom that said ATOMIC POWER. Its beam was so bright that everyone had to look away when I turned it on. As I shined the light under Duff, we all tilted forward, blinking against the glare. I had to clear my throat repeatedly, and the old lady held her breath. Pumpkin whined as Stump gasped, "It's gone."

"Liar!" Biz squeaked. Pushing Stump aside, he crowded forward to see for himself.

"Probably never there," the old man said.

"It better have been," the old lady warned.

"My aunt's going to kill me," Biz squeaked, crowding so close that his snout almost touched Duff. As Biz inched closer, his tail whipped back and forth so hard that Pumpkin snapped at it.

Scared, Stump reared away from Pumpkin's fangs, upsetting Biz's balance as he did.

"Don't!" Biz shouted.

Biz fell sideways, colliding with Jim Dandy, who crashed into the old man, who lost his grip on the marble arm, which slipped off the saucepot, causing Duff to topple toward Biz.

"Look out!"

That must have been me shouting. I don't know who else it could have been. Everybody else was busy shouting a different warning.

"Stop!"

"No!"

"Fools!"

"Woof!"

Biz, Jim Dandy, and Duff smacked into one another.

forty one

THE MISSING FEATHER

Just like that, Biz and Jim Dandy were stone. The stone didn't start where Biz's snout collided with Duff's ribs, or Jim Dandy's paw landed on Duff's shoulder, and spread from there. It didn't go in stages. It happened all at once, like a flash, except that there wasn't any light or sound or even the slightest shimmer. It just was. Neither troll even had time to cry out. They'd become the same crumbly yellowish sandstone as all the others.

Their crickets got it too. They clung to Jim Dandy's hair and Biz's shoulder, more stone than bug and unable to lie about a single thing.

One thing they could have lied about was the whereabouts of the stone feather. Stump was right about that much; it wasn't hidden under Duff. We could see that much for sure now that Duff had toppled forward. There was a stone beneath Duff, but not one that looked anything like a feather. It was square shaped, with some writing scratched on it. Using the marble arm's fingers, the old man bumped it away from Duff, where the old lady could reach it with the stone glove. We crowded around her to read:

IOU

B. DEEPTHINK

Little as we had to say, you might have thought we'd all been turned to stone ourselves. But finally we found our voices.

"How'd that get there?" the old man crossly said.

"No trouble for Bodacious to put it there," the old lady answered. "She's mostly stone anyway."

"But how'd she know the feather was here?" Stump asked, rubbing his eyes as if it might change what he saw.

I knew the answer to that, though I certainly wished I didn't.

"Duke," I said grimly. "But what's she want with it?"

"To set a trap," the old lady supposed.

"For who?" Stump asked.

"Whoever comes after the feather."

"Why in the world would she want us?" Stump said.

"For mining," the old man guessed with admiration. "Isn't she slick?"

"Oh, now wait a minute," Stump objected, sounding just sick about it. "That's not right. We already said no to being miners."

"Bodacious Deepthink doesn't take no for an answer," the old man said. "The question is, what are you going to do about it?"

"The only thing we can," the old lady answered. "Go get the feather."

forty two

RELIABLE ST. JOHN

We headed back to Trolls & Things to rest until nightfall, when we would tackle Bo. The old man and Pumpkin dropped us off at the rowboat, which, minus Jim Dandy and Biz, wasn't anywhere near as crowded. The extra room didn't make Stump any happier, though. He missed his partners, he still had to hide out under a flowery hat, and his conscience flared up. Most of the cruise back he badmouthed himself for not having told me where their stone feather had been.

"I was afraid you'd get yourself turned to stone," he explained.

"Forget it," I repeated for the umpteenth time.

"Do you really mean it?"

"Mostly."

That quieted Stump for a hundred yards or so, when he started peppering his cricket with questions. The cricket, whose name was Reliable St. John, burrowed into Stump's leafy hair, refusing to answer.

"What kind of lucky cricket are you?" Stump demanded to know. "My partners are stone."

"A very sensible one," the old lady answered for the lucky cricket. "One who's not too eager to see Bodacious Deepthink again."

"Why not?" Stump said.

"Because she's so nice," Reliable St. John piped up.

That lie silenced Stump for fifty yards, after which he asked in a small, small voice, "Do you really know where my father is?"

"Of course not," Reliable said. "None of the other fathers either."

Satisfied that at least Reliable St. John could lead him to his father, Stump shut up.

By noon we were entering the old lady's store through a back door that led down a hallway crowded with crates and boxes stamped with labels like PRODUCT OF TIBET or KEEP FROZEN 1000 YEARS or MIDNIGHT GLASSWARE. Stepping through another door, we found ourselves in a small kitchen, where the old lady served me peaches and cream, twice, and gave Stump the okay to dip into the tub holding willow cats. Reliable St. John was given a small leaf of lettuce to dine on.

Then naps. After promising to keep his mouth shut, Stump was allowed to conk out in a bathtub filled with minnows. Reliable St. John was tucked away in a bamboo cage that was hung from a rafter. In case the cricket had any tricks in mind, the old lady asked her raccoon friend, Princess Trudy, to stand guard below the cage. My guest room was a dry bathtub filled with blankets and heart-shaped pillows.

"I don't even known your name," I said, wanting to say something grateful as the old lady tucked me in.

"I don't either," she said with a sad smile. "It's gone."

"Gone?" I sat up. "Gone where?"

The old lady smoothed my hair with a soft, comforting touch of her hand. "It seems like just yesterday that your grandfather asked me that question too."

"So what'd you tell him?"

"That I didn't think he could be trusted to keep a secret."

"He hasn't been known to keep many," I agreed, trying with all my might not to worry about him or Aunt Phyllis, Uncle Norm, Duff, and even—a little—Jim Dandy and Biz.

Tapping a finger on my chest to show how serious this was, she said, "You must promise never to tell anyone."

"I'll do my best."

"From what I've seen," she said, lifting her hand away, "I couldn't ask for more."

A look far away as the moon settled over her eyes then. Whatever she was remembering widened her smile but deepened her sadness.

"My name's gone into a spell," she said at last. "A spell that lets magic work along this stretch of river. If it wasn't for the spell, the magic folk around here would have all been drowned a century ago by these modern times."

"How can you be drowned by time?" I frowned.

"Very easily," she sighed, turning away from me to gaze out a window at the river. "A long while ago, magic worked anywhere in this world. Magic folk lived where they wanted, practiced magic as they liked. Not at all like these days, when magic sputters and fizzes at best. Just try walking through a brick wall. You'll see what I mean. Today there's only a few enchanted pockets left here and there, protected by spells that shield them from the passing of time. We dare not stick a toe outside the spell protecting us or we freeze up worse than ice."

"Even in the summer?"

"Especially in the summer. I'm talking of a different kind of cold than you're thinking of, my dear. Cold caused by time is a cold that you feel on the inside. More like loneliness than ice. And when any of us feels it, we can't help but burn ourselves up trying to keep warm. Usually we magic folk stay warm by migrating, like birds in the fall, but those of us along the river here have been left behind, stranded."

"How'd that happen?"

"Miscalculations," she said with a grim look that discouraged follow-up questions.

"But where do you migrate to?" I asked.

"Other worlds, where the time for magic is now."

I nodded slowly, thinking of those other worlds until a thought occurred to me.

"If you're like the birds, does that mean you come back in the spring?"

"Oh, yes," the old lady said, brightening. "That's what we're waiting for. Our spring, when magic will work all over this world again. It's coming, but for now we're so cooped up along the river that you can hardly turn around without bumping into a hex, a curse, or general witchery of some kind. In the olden days, when we had more elbow room, magic folk weren't so quick to anger, but packed in tight as we are now, well, it's gotten out of hand lately. And Bodacious Deepthink's the worst of all. That's one of the reasons I need to pay her a visit, to bring her down a peg or two. Maybe then she'll behave a little better. So there you have it. That's what happened to my name, and the name of every other blue-wing along this stretch of river."

"But can't you take another name?"

"That would only weaken the spell," she said, patting me on the head as if it was kind of me to want to help. "And now you better try to get some rest."

"Will I need it?"

"I'm afraid you will," she answered, lifting some sparkly dust from her apron pocket and sprinkling it on my eyes. Once again I felt as though I were slowly falling, just like at the wagon wheel bridge, but this time I was falling asleep.

forty three

NETTIE'S MESSAGE

The next thing I knew, the old lady was blowing gently across my face, her breath sweet as fresh cider. Late-afternoon sunlight slanted through the store windows, so only a few hours had passed, but a week of sleep couldn't have refreshed me more. I popped right up.

"Is there anything that dust can't do?" I asked.

"Quite a bit, actually, but for small kinds of magic that involve falling of one kind or another—even falling asleep—it's quite handy. Put enough on and it's good for raising things too, 'cause of course that's just falling done backwards. But now we have to get moving. It's getting late, if we're going to get that stone feather before Bo forgets where she put it. First off, we need to have a word about trolls."

I nodded to show that she had my attention.

"I may not be able to save you if we get caught," the old lady continued. "Bodacious Deepthink's not called the Great Rock Troll for nothing."

"Are you trying to scare me?"

"I'm doing my best," she said with a chuckle that was more friendly than mean. "Before we get started, I need to be certain that you want to go through with this."

"It doesn't matter if I'm scared or not," I told her. "My grandpa and the others need that feather, and Duke may be a pill, but I don't think he belongs down there."

All of what I'd said was true enough, but there was one last thing I'd left unsaid—maybe even to myself—that was even more true. Where else was I ever going to get a chance to stand up to Bodacious Deepthink? The old lady had said that was the only way to undo the Great Rock Troll's curse, which meant that it was the only way to find out if I was once a river troll.

The answers to some questions can change your whole life, and this answer seemed scary enough to be one of them. I wasn't exactly sure that I wanted to know the answer, but my once being a river troll would sure explain some things. Big things, like how I measured up so different from my sisters or felt so good around turtles and toads and such. And little things too, like hating vegetables and almost feeling sort of comfortable around Stump.

"Very well," the old lady answered with a satisfied nod that said she'd judged me right. "Then we'd better gather ourselves and our supplies, starting with our guide." With that, she collected the cage holding Reliable St. John. "There's tunnels all over where we're headed, and this cricket's been through them before."

"I haven't, I haven't, I haven't," Reliable St. John sang from his cage.

"Now where did I put that rope?" the old lady said, ignoring Reliable's chorus.

"We need rope?" I asked.

"For tripping." She hunted up a white rope, which she wrapped around and around her waist until it looked like a wide belt. "Rock trolls take a long time to get back up. You've still got a good riddle handy, right?"

"I guess so."

"Let's hear it." The old lady made an out-with-it motion.

So I recited the riddle that Two-cents Eel-tongue had made up. To my surprise, the old lady kissed her fingertips the way a chef does when a dish tastes just right.

"Perfect," she said. "Pure river troll, which is exactly what you need to flummox a rock troll." She rubbed her hands together in anticipation. "All right, except for a couple of bags of gravel, I'd say we're about ready. Have you ever used a slingshot?"

"Once. Before my cousin took it away."

"You'll need some practice, then."

She and I spent an hour knocking empty pop cans off a counter with a slingshot. By then Stump had joined us, but he shied away from an offered slingshot, refusing to trust anything made by a human hand. The old lady was a deadeye, but I broke a few things. After an hour or so, she declared I was ready as I'd ever be.

"What exactly are we going to be shooting at?" I asked.

"Lanterns."

"Glad to hear it," I said. "I didn't think these would be much good against Bodacious Deepthink."

"My dear," the old lady confided, "there's not a thing in my store would hurt Bo. That's why it's best if she never even knows we've been there until we're gone."

"What are the chances of that?" I asked, kind of quavery-like.

She answered my question by saying, "Maybe I better have a look into your eyes again."

Without thinking, I snapped my eyes shut, afraid. What if she saw a river troll that bore a striking resemblance to me? But then Stump stepped close to whisper in my ear.

"You shouldn't ever pass up a chance to look in a fairy's eyes."

"Why not?" I whispered back.

"They say you can see the answer to whatever's troubling you."

"Is that true?" I said, raising my voice to the old lady. My eyes were still shut.

"It's been known to happen," she answered modestly.

Taking a deep breath, I popped open my eyes, and the old lady leaned forward until we were nose to nose.

"What do you see?" I was ready to flinch.

"Still crickets," she said, amused by my brave face. "Maybe what you see is more important."

So I looked.

"It's that young lady again," I said, relieved. "The one in the sunbonnet. Who is she, anyway?"

"Does she look familiar?"

"Sort of."

"That's because you two look a good deal alike. She's your Great-Great-Great-Grandmother Nettie."

Gazing closer, I could see it was true. The girl in the sunbonnet did look remarkably like me, though several years older.

"How do you know all this?" I asked.

"Oh, I knew Nettie as a girl. We came upriver on the same steamer—the *Rose Melinda*. I'm not at all surprised she's come back to help you. Family always mattered a good deal to her. What's she doing right now?"

"Standing on the bank of a sandbar," I said, looking more closely. "Writing something in the wet sand with a stick."

"Can you read it?"

"It's upside down."

"Concentrate."

I did. This was what I saw:

ˑdn ʎɹɹnɥ oʇ ɯᴉɥ llǝ┴

˙pʎolℲ ɹoɟ ʞs∀

Finally I pieced it together by mouthing the letters out loud, one by one, until they made sense as words.

Ask for Floyd.
Tell him to hurry up.

After repeating it to myself two or three times, I read it louder for the others.

"Who's Floyd?" I asked.

"If memory serves," the old lady said, "you have a great-great-great-granduncle named Floyd Bridgewater."

"That's right!" I remembered. "Grandpa B told us about him. He grew a horn and disappeared. But how am I going to ask for him? He's been gone for a hundred years or better."

"I don't know," the old lady said thoughtfully, "but something tells me we'll find out."

forty four

STUMP'S MESSAGE

Do you mind if I have a look?" Stump asked the old lady. "In your eyes, I mean. Please?"

He really did have exceptionally good manners for a troll, and good manners are awfully hard to turn down, especially when they're least expected. The old lady waved him closer.

The way Stump approached her, he might have been trying to look at the sun. He squinted at the old lady's eyes a long time before stumbling back, in shock.

"What is it?" I asked. "What'd you see?"

"Your cousin." He shook his head to clear his vision.

"Huh?"

"All I see is your cousin," Stump repeated forlornly. "How's he going to help with my troubles?"

"You're sure it was Duke?" I said.

"He's pretty hard to miss, don't you think?"

"Was he doing anything?" the old lady asked.

"Not that I could see," Stump complained. "Other than eating. He sure wasn't writing me any messages in the sand, if that's what you mean."

"Where was he?" I asked.

"In the dark."

"What was he eating?" I was hoping to find something that might cheer Stump up and be useful at the same time.

"It was too dark to tell. All I could see for sure was that he was chewing and chewing and chewing."

"Was he alone?" the old lady asked.

"I couldn't tell."

"Was he still a rhinoceros?"

"Yes, yes," Stump answered, turning away dejectedly. "Just the way we left him."

After that, the old lady fed us supper, dishing out raspberries and cream to me, Princess Trudy, and herself; more willow cats for Stump, who remained in a funk; and an apple seed or two for Reliable St. John. When done eating, the old lady seated Stump and me at the store's big front window to watch for her brother. Behind us, she went about closing up her shop. She sprinkled dry food on the fish tanks, flipped an enormous hourglass, and wound up the engine of a toy train. The train chugged off down wooden tracks, hauling a line of cars filled with sunflower seeds. Just before the train disappeared into a wall hole, a fat mouse, dressed in a blue conductor's uniform, stepped onto the caboose's back platform to wave farewell. The old lady waved back and stepped over to a refrigerator, where she filled her apron pockets with sparkly powder from a canister. Then she joined us at the front window.

Nobody felt like talking, especially not Reliable St. John. The old lady had removed him from his cage and set him on Stump's shoulder, saying we needed to travel light, which meant no cages. The closest any of us came to talking was grinding our teeth. Stump and I took turns doing that.

Finally, near dusk, headlights pulled up in front of the store and a horn honked twice. The old lady hustled us out the door to her brother, who had driven over to Big Rock.

"Farmer Bailey's pasture?" the old man guessed.

"By the back way," the old lady said. "And when you hit the Sweeny place, would you mind turning off your headlights?"

"It seems to me," the old man groused, "that I'm always driving you somewhere with my headlights off."

forty five

FARMER BAILEY'S PASTURE

We turned off the highway onto a narrow blacktop road that wound up the far side of a long valley. Just one night ago I'd been carted up the same valley while hanging from a pole. Curving away from the woods and the rock face that Bodacious Deepthink had stepped out of, the road continued climbing.

A little past an abandoned farmhouse, which must have been the Sweeny place, the old man flicked off his headlights and we drove silently on in the gathering darkness. The higher the road went, the slower the old man drove, till at last we were barely creeping. Glancing at his hands on the steering wheel, I noticed a silver ring identical to the one the old lady wore. The ring was frosting up, but when I looked at the old man's high forehead, I saw beads of sweat. What the old lady had said about magic folk burning up if they left the valley came back to me. But still the old man drove on. Just below a final crest out of the valley, the old lady said, "This should do."

Her brother dropped us off beside a black ditch, turned his pickup around, and headed back down with Princess Trudy and Pumpkin, whose whiskers were frosty. When passing us, he rolled down his window.

"You've still got that stone glove?" he asked.

"Of course." The old lady patted a bulge in her apron pocket.

"Well, don't lose it."

And off the old man drove. I was hoping the pickup would lift off the ground and fly away—it did belong to a blue-wing fairy, after all—but it stuck to the road. If the old man turned his headlights back on, I never saw them.

"It won't be long now," the old lady told us.

"What are we waiting for?"

"Farmer Bailey. He knows the way, or has always claimed to. We'll see."

She walked up to the barbed-wire fence fronting the road, crawled underneath it, and motioned for me and Stump to follow. I didn't have any trouble skinning under the wire, but it was a tight fit for Stump. First he tried sliding on his stomach, but his tail stuck up too high. Then he tried on his back, but his gut wouldn't go. Finally the old lady tossed a handful of sparkly dust on him and floated him over.

We stopped right on the other side of the fence in a thinly wooded pasture. So that he wouldn't drift away, Stump clung to an oak standing barely twenty yards from the top of the ridge. While hanging on, he grumped about a chill in his tail. Though the night was warmish, I could hear the old lady's teeth chattering from time to time too, and every once in a while Reliable St. John would say with a shiver, "Don't start a fire. Don't start a fire. Don't start a fire."

Which let you know how cold he was.

Beneath these small complaints, I kept imagining that I heard low and distant voices. Finally I couldn't take it any longer and whispered, "Who's talking?"

The old lady pointed to the matted brown grass beneath our feet and whispered back, "Our friends."

forty six

SMACK NOODLES & GUMBOIL SOUP

An hour passed. If I told you it got darker during that hour, I don't see how you could believe me. A lump of coal didn't have anything on that night.

The voices kept jabbering below us. They might have been singing or arguing. From the little I knew of trolls, it was probably both.

Finally two headlights came slowly bouncing over the crown of the hill. With them came a noisy tractor pulling a hay wagon that we crept after, stumbling in the dark. Fifty yards later the tractor came to a stop near a clump of trees that dipped lower than the surrounding pasture.

"A-ha," said the old lady.

When the rock in a place is limestone, like around here, it's easily hollowed out by water. There's hardly anything groundwater loves to eat more than limestone. Sometimes so much limestone gets washed away that top layers of rock collapse, making a sinkhole, and that's where the clump of trees was growing, in a sinkhole. Of course what goes hand in hand with sinkholes and hollowed-out limestone is caves.

By the light of the tractor, Farmer Bailey used a hand-held hook to snag bales of hay and drop them down an opening at the sinkhole's center.

"What's he doing?" I whispered.

"Paying tribute."

"I thought tribute got paid with gold and things."

"Bo prefers hay," the old lady answered. "And if she doesn't get it, the first thing Farmer Bailey knows, he's missing some cattle or sheep."

"What's Bo want with hay?"

"Shhh."

The voices beneath us had inched closer.

As soon as Farmer Bailey left, we crept into the sinkhole, which sat in the pasture like a bowl the size of a house. Inside the bowl was grass, moss, a small grove of stunted oaks, and—near the center— a hole the shape of a narrow bathtub that gave off a weak, purplish white glow. Peeking over the hole's edge, we could see a pair of rock trolls loading hay bales on an old two-wheeled cart. They were bickering, and we were now close enough to catch most of what they had to say.

"Smack noodles and gumboil soup. I'm sick of 'em."

"Watch your tongue or it might go missing."

"All I'm saying is, her highness could snag us a calf or piggy now and then, couldn't she? For variety. But no, she wants this hay for her pets, so Farmer Bailey's livestock is off-limits. Is that fair?"

"Maybe yes. Maybe no. It ain't for the likes of us to . . ."

About then I quit listening. Why? Harnessed to the cart was Duke.

I recognized my cousin by the black zipper coat still hanging on him. Though the coat's seams had split open to make room for the rhinoceros he'd become, it still clung to him around the shoulders, like a cape. He was busy munching on a bale of hay set before him. Back home a brass band would have started playing if he so much as touched his greens.

Two shooting-star lanterns on poles lit the scene. Around the cart stretched a shadowy cavern that looked big enough to swallow a whale.

With the cart filled, the trolls led Duke away by spreading handfuls of hay every few feet in front of him. Progress was slow, but eventually they moved out of sight, and the lantern light below us paled.

"We'll float down," the old lady said.

"We will?"

She reached into a pocket and sprinkled me with dust that felt like fine sand, only alive and sparkly. Right away I turned sort of bubbly and light-footed. Looking down, I saw why. I wasn't touching the ground.

"You'll need a rock." The old lady handed me a head-size one.

After that, she gave Stump another sprinkle of dust, gave him a rock, and pushed him toward the hole too.

"I'm not scared, I'm not scared, I'm not scared," Reliable St. John chanted from Stump's shoulder.

The old lady pointed a finger at him, shutting him up, but now Stump was balking. He leaned over the hole, gazing down into the purple glow as if facing his doom.

"It's the only way to save Biz and Jim Dandy and find your father," the old lady reminded him.

"I know," he squeaked miserably.

Touching the middle of his back, the old lady gave him a shove. It was a tight fit, but he went down the hole without a sound, though his mouth was open almost as wide as his eyes.

The old lady tossed some dust above herself, snatched up a rock, and hopped into the hole after him. I followed, knowing better than to start thinking about what I was doing.

Down and down we went, falling slow as a balloon that's thinking about going up.

Right away I could smell trolls, all mildewy and sweaty and moldy. It got colder. Damper. But that was all kids' stuff compared to the view in front of me.

The spot where Farmer Bailey dropped his hay bales was the shallow part of the cavern. At the other end, lit up by shooting-star lanterns, the cavern opened into a space big enough to swallow several pods of whales. I could see trolls swinging pickaxes and hauling rock in wheelbarrows, and all the while they were pushing, shoving, and shouting. The cavern was riddled with holes, false starts to the moon, I supposed.

Right at the center of all the action stood Bodacious Deepthink, the Great Rock Troll herself, looking two or three times bigger underground. That was probably because she was standing up straighter and wearing a construction hat, along with her tiger-striped nylon outfit.

Crouching beside her was Jim Dandy's father, Double-knot Eel-tongue, with a blueprint spread over his back. Looking from the blueprint to her miners, Bo belted out an angry stream of orders.

"Faster!"

"Deeper!"

"No snacking!"

The Great Rock Troll kept spinning this way and that, and every time she shifted, she expected Double-knot to move with her. But being asked to scurry around on all fours wasn't the worst of Double-knot's problems, not by a long shot.

Every so often Bo needed a breather from all her shouting and braying. Whenever that happened, Double-knot was supposed to rush behind her and become a stool. As she sat down on him, he sagged and creaked and groaned, all of which tickled Bodacious Deepthink no end.

But the sight that stole my breath away was a large rock corral that was separated from the rest of the cave by an underground stream. The trolls were leading the hay cart across a short stone bridge to that corral. Milling around on the other side of that bridge were twenty to thirty bullies, a whole herd of them. They all looked as though wishing they'd never picked on anyone smaller than themselves in their whole life. How could I tell they were bullies? They were all rhinoceroses.

forty seven

COO·COO·BA·ROO

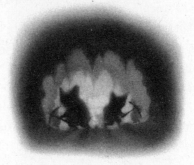

If you ever land in a cave full of rock trolls, remember not to breathe deep. The air trapped in that cave hasn't been around any roses.

The other reason you dare not breathe is that rock trolls might hear you. In a cave, everything echoes, and rock trolls have ears the size of lumpy baseball mitts. Luckily, the cave we were sinking into was so full of sounds—ringing pickaxes, shouting rock trolls, snorting rhinos, chirping cave crickets—that the thumps we made upon landing were hardly noticed at all.

"You hear something?" grumbled a rock troll pushing a wheelbarrow.

"Moonbeams," scoffed his partner without even stopping.

The old lady waved us behind a stalagmite and whispered, "We'll wait here until dawn."

It wasn't a night I'll forget soon enough. There was no mistaking rock trolls for anything else I'd ever heard of, not even river trolls. If you have any boulders in your family, you'll know what I'm talking about. The trolls before us were bald and bumpy and had very little bend to them. Heavy as their feet were, they shuffled everywhere.

The liveliest thing about them was their eyes, which sparkled like split diamonds in the lantern light.

The cavern floor shook with their digging. They yelled about everything, then had to shout louder to be heard above their own echoes. Smashing rocks made them laugh. Fighting with each other made them happy. Lighting fuses made them try to dance, which usually led to a fall. They hauled rock until they broke for supper, or whatever you call a meal taken in the middle of the night. When they ate, their slurping echoed like breakers on an ocean beach.

Back at work, they started burping. There were fumes.

At last, morning. Our end of the cave began to lighten to a mousy gray, thanks to the hole in Farmer Bailey's pasture. The trolls noticed the change almost at once and dropped everything but their grumbling. The bunch closest to us carried on like this:

"We'll never reach the moon at this rate."

"Somebody ought to go up there and smash that sun."

"You ignoramus. We don't have any ladders that high."

"Couldn't we build one?"

"When, on our day off?"

Which started a whole new round of bickering, for they never got a day off — not even holidays or birthdays. Slowly, they drifted off to holes and crevices for a long day's sleep. Two or three trolls stumbled around covering up lanterns with burlap bags that said BIG ROCK FEED AND SEED. The shooting stars winked out one by one until the only light in the cave was the pale glow from the hole in Farmer Bailey's pasture.

"We'll wait until they're sound asleep," the old lady whispered.

Before I could ask how long that would take, a voice filled the cavern with a lullaby that was soft and sweet as a chorus of nightingales. Peeking around my stalagmite, I saw Bodacious Deepthink singing with her arms outstretched, eyes closed, and bat earrings fluttering about her head.

The moon is down below us
Singing to us all.
    coo-coo-ba-roo
        coo-coo-ba-roo

Just close your eyes and listen.
You're sure to hear its call.
    coo-coo-ba-roo
        coo-coo-ba-roo

You'll find yourself smiling.
You're going to take a fall.
    coo-coo-ba-roo
        coo-coo-ba-roo

The day we finally reach it
We're going to have a ball.
    coo-coo-ba-roo
      ba-roo   *ba-roo*
        who-coo
            coo-coo-coo
            coo-coo

By the time she'd crooned her way through the lullaby twice, the snores in the cave sounded like a thousand sloppy geysers. Double-knot Eel-tongue had collapsed in a heap at her feet.

Leaving Jim Dandy's father right where he lay, Bodacious Deepthink clumped to the stone bridge that arched over the under-water stream and led to the rhinos. Halfway across she flopped down sideways with a thud. You could hear her humming the lullaby to herself until she too fell asleep, blocking the only way to the rhinos. Her snores were louder and dreamier than all the other hissing and fizzing that filled the place.

"How do we get around her?" I whispered.

"Easy," the old lady said.

When we started walking, I saw what she meant. My feet still held some of the bubbles that had let me float down from Farmer Bailey's pasture. With a helping boost from the old lady, Stump and I leaped the stream in one bound. Once across, the old lady motioned for Stump to hang back in the shadows.

"You might spook 'em."

Then she and I stepped up to the corral's rock fence, which came up to my chin.

From up close, the rhinos that I could see weren't plump, and their wrinkly skins looked ready to slip off. Remnants of clothes clung to their pointy ears, bony legs, and knobby ankles. They wore socks without heels, flattened caps, and tattered pant legs and shirtsleeves, though never the whole pants or shirt. One rhino wore a black eye patch that looked left over from Halloween, and two girl rhinos had dabs of fingernail polish on their hooves—lime green and ketchup red. Bodacious Deepthink's lullaby hadn't soothed the herd at all. They stood paired off, butting heads, going horn to horn, with much pushing, grunting, and name-calling, all done in hushed whispers so as not to wake the Great Rock Troll. What we heard was pretty standard stuff for bullies:

"I'm bigger."

"Than a peach pit."

"One step closer and I'll peach pit you."

"One step? I didn't know you could count that high."

"Try me and see."

Some rhinos were claiming to be geniuses or related to royalty or in possession of a secret map that showed the way out of the cave. In fact, several bragged up secret maps. The way they were all jostling and pushing and milling around made it impossible to pick Duke out of the crowd, so finally I gave up looking and called out in a hushed voice, "Duke."

Nobody paid attention.

"Duke," I called again.

Finally, the oldest-looking rhino in the herd hobbled over, snuffling all the way. His wrinkled gray skin hung on him like draperies. His horn was chipped, and the hair in his ears stuck out like thornbushes. Squashed atop his head was a shapeless hat that had aged worse than him, if that was possible.

Since rhinos have such poor eyesight, he had to stick his face, horn and all, over the stone fence to see us. After several deep sniffs and a lot of blinking, he shook his head from side to side, as if he still couldn't believe what what he was seeing, and said, "Is that you, Nettie?"

forty eight

FLOYD TITUS BRIDGEWATER

How could a rhinoceros trapped in a cave mistake me for my great-great-great-grandmother? The answer came from the old lady, who advised me, "Ask if he's Floyd."

I didn't need to ask, though. The rhino heard her and said, "Floyd Titus Bridgewater, at your service, ladies. At your service."

And he made a short bow that started several of the closer rhinos ragging on him:

"Would you look at old Floyd."

"Thinks he's a gentleman."

"The old fool."

The old lady nudged me forward. "Tell him who you are."

"My name is Claire Antoinette Bridgewater," I said, feeling shy enough to turn formal. "Nettie Bridgewater was my great-great-great-grandmother."

"Now, how can that be?" Floyd asked. "I've only been down here a few weeks. Months at the most."

"I think it's safe to say it's been longer than that," the old lady said.

"Who are you?" Uncle Floyd demanded, perturbed.

"Friend of the family," the old lady breezed on, "and Nettie's sent you a message."

"What kind of message?" Uncle Floyd turned cautious.

"Well," I started, after the old lady nudged me again, "she said to tell you to hurry up."

At that, the old rhino muttered considerably, saying to himself, "Sounds like Nettie, all right." Raising his head to us, he added, "She was a bossy little thing, worse than a princess. Well, if you're her great-great-great-granddaughter, I guess that means my fool brother went ahead and got hitched to her. Serves him right, I'd say." He carried on that way until he got around to saying gruffly, "I guess that makes me your uncle."

"Don't worry," I declared, standing up to him. "I won't tell anyone."

"Likewise," he grumped.

But I could tell I'd won him over just a bit by showing some backbone. Dealing with Duke had taught me a thing or two after all, at least when it came to bullies. Remembering how Grandpa B liked nothing better than being questioned about bygone days, I asked, "But how have you lasted down here so long?"

"Sentimental reasons," he confided. "I'm the first bully Bodacious Deepthink ever caught, so she likes to keep me around. But enough about me. What in the world are you two doing down here? It's not a proper place for ladies."

"I need to talk to my cousin Duke," I said.

"Which Duke is that?"

"How many have you got?" the old lady asked him.

"Three. Four if you count the lunkhead got dumped off last night."

"That's the lunk we want," the old lady said.

"He's over there eating himself silly." Uncle Floyd pointed with his horn. "You sure he's a Bridgewater?"

Off to one side, cloaked by shadows, stood a rhino munching away on Farmer Bailey's hay. The black zipper jacket hanging around his neck said it was Duke. He was fatter and shinier than the rest of the herd, and I didn't see any way we'd ever float him out of the hole in Farmer Bailey's field. Even the rhinos who were nothing but skin and bones didn't look like they could be squeezed out that way.

"Sure as can be," I muttered, wishing otherwise. "His mother's a Bridgewater."

"You here to spring him?"

"That's the plan," the old lady said.

"How?"

"Knock out the lights and run."

"Some plan," Uncle Floyd pooh-poohed.

"We'll listen to anything better."

"You know," Uncle Floyd admitted after some thought, "these trolls aren't exactly packed with brains. Maybe your idea would work. If you know the way out, that is."

"We knew the way in, didn't we?"

"I guess you did," Uncle Floyd agreed, turning hopeful. "Take me too?"

"We'll take anyone who wants to go."

"That'd be all twenty-nine of us," Uncle Floyd declared.

"So round 'em up," the old lady said.

Uncle Floyd hobbled off to do just that, and within minutes we had twenty-eight horns pointing at us. The only horn not jabbed our way belonged to the Duke who was my cousin. He stayed off to the side, facing our general direction but too busy chowing down on hay to pay us full attention. The other rhinos gave us a hard once-over, saying things like:

"They don't look like much to me."

"What are they selling?"

"Why, they couldn't lead us out of a paper bag."

But Uncle Floyd stood up for us. "This scrawny one's my niece, so mind your manners. And who's had a better offer?"

The rhinos quieted then, for of course they hadn't had any other offers at all.

"I'm only going to say this once," the old lady whispered, "so you better get him too."

She pointed at Duke.

Four rhinos charged over and convinced Duke to join us in nothing flat. They weren't too gentle about it either, but then Duke wasn't too eager to be parted from his hay. Once my cousin recovered his dignity, he leaned his weak rhino eyes over the fence as far as he could for a good solid look at me. His mouth dropped open, with bits of hay falling out, as he said, "I thought I was finally rid of you."

"We're trying to get you home," I sassed right back.

"Who says I want to go?" Duke blustered. "I like it down here just dandy. I've made new friends."

"No, you haven't," Uncle Floyd told him.

"And there's plenty to eat," Duke went on.

"As much as you want." Uncle Floyd's tone made it clear that Duke was a fool for wanting it.

"So who asked for any help?" Duke wanted to know. "Naw, I'm staying right here."

"Not for long, you're not," said Uncle Floyd. "Not the way you're packing down the hay."

"Huh?" Duke stopped in midchew.

"You heard me. Why do you think you're the only one eating?"

"You're not hungry?" Duke guessed, realizing as he spoke how dumb it sounded. The rib cage of every rhino around him was easy to see as the bars of a birdcage. How could they not be absolutely famished?

"You're darn tooting we're not hungry," Uncle Floyd scoffed. "We've seen what happens if you are. First you get all plump and juicy, then it's snack time."

"What's wrong with a little snack?" Duke protested.

"Nothing. Unless *you're* the snack."

"Now, wait a minute," Duke said, gagging. "You guys told me to eat!"

Suddenly all the other rhinos lowered their heads, unable to look at Duke.

"Now you know exactly how many friends all of us have down here," Uncle Floyd told him.

There was a whole lot of head hanging and hoof shuffling as we pictured the Great Rock Troll tying on her bib and getting out her best china. Sniffles broke out here and there. The old lady shook them out of their tailspin by saying, "Fortunately for you, everyone's entitled to a second chance. It's one of the basic laws of the universe."

They all crowded closer with that news, even Duke, who squinted toward the old lady, and said, "Who's that? It sounds like that crazy old bat who tried to drown me."

"Watch it," I warned. "She's here to help you."

"Said the spider to the fly."

We went back and forth in our usual way until the old lady called out softly, "Stump, maybe you better come up here. He might listen to you."

"Who?" Duke couldn't believe his new ears.

"Me," Stump said, stepping out of the shadows.

One look at Stump sent all the other rhinos backpedaling, and reverse isn't an easy direction for anyone with four legs. A considerable pileup was followed by snorting and heartfelt name-calling—all whispered, of course. Duke, alone, stood his ground, unable to believe his luck.

"Is it really you?" Duke asked. "I knew you guys would come for me. I just knew it. But where's Jim Dandy? Where's Biz? What's the plan?"

"Stone," Stump said. "Both of 'em. That's why we're here. We need the stone feather Bodacious Deepthink took from your house."

"No you don't, no you don't, no you don't," Reliable St. John sang from Stump's shoulder.

"But I don't know anything about that," Duke squawked.

"Oh, come off it," Uncle Floyd said. "Every rhino here heard you tell Bo where to find it. Why, she wouldn't even have known about that feather if you hadn't told her."

"I was desperate," Duke whined.

"Not to mention pathetic," Uncle Floyd added.

Other rhinos shared unflattering opinions of Duke until the old lady interrupted.

"Do you know where the feather is now?" she asked.

"I saw her put it in her vest pocket." Duke sniffled.

"That's it, then," the old lady stated. "Once I get the feather, we'll be getting out of here."

"And just how are we doing that?" the rhino with the eye patch wanted to know.

"With a trick or two."

"They better be good ones," Uncle Floyd said. "The last rhino who got caught making a break for it got tucked into popovers."

"I don't trust her," Duke whimpered.

"You'd rather trust Bodacious Deepthink?" I asked.

"Let him," called a rhino from in back.

"Not me," said another.

"His neck."

"Quiet!" the old lady whispered. "My helpers and I have work to do, and we need to do it while Bo's asleep. When we get back, I want you all ready to charge across the bridge."

"Bo's there!" There were several gasps.

"She won't be when the time comes," vowed the old lady.

forty nine

GETTING THE STONE FEATHER

We left the rhinos without answering any more questions, though there were plenty of them flying around. Once out of earshot of the herd, the old lady held up a hand for everyone to halt.

"Which tunnel takes us up top?" she asked, speaking to Reliable St. John.

"That one," the cave cricket answered from Stump's shoulder. He dipped an antennae toward a tiny tunnel far across the cavern. "Try that one."

"Way over there?" The old lady lifted an amused eyebrow. "Are you sure?"

"That's the one."

"I was hoping it would be," the old lady said. Turning her back on the tiny tunnel, she pointed at a large one directly opposite it. "How about that one? Would that get us home too?"

"Better skip that one." Reliable St. John sounded hopeful that she wouldn't. "It's a dead end."

We now faced a tunnel big around as a school bus but without a hint of yellow anywhere. The only color to that tunnel was black. Its mouth was barred with stalagmites and stalactites that looked like sharp teeth in bad need of a dentist, worse need of floss. But the two front teeth had been punched out, leaving a hole big enough to scrape through, though Bodacious Deepthink probably had to turn sideways and hold her breath to make it. A bigger give-away was the path leading up to the tunnel. Shiny and worn, it led all the way from the stone bridge where Bodacious Deepthink slept.

"That's the one," the old lady said, satisfied that she'd sifted the truth out of the cricket's lies. "Now I want you three to collect a lantern and go stand by that tunnel. Leave the lantern covered until I get the rhinos headed your way, then whip off the cover and give the glass a good rap to get the star glowing. These bullies will need something bright to aim for."

"But"—Stump faltered—"where are you going to be?"

"Why, getting the feather," she joshed, trying to make it sound like a walk in the park. "And if I can't get back to you, just go on without me. You'll have the cricket to guide you, and I'll meet you up top."

The old lady sounded way too cheery to be reassuring. To make matters darker, nobody could think of anything else to say, so with nods and gulps all around, we parted. When the old lady could no longer hear us, Reliable St. John whispered to Stump, "Wrong way, wrong way, wrong way." At least that much was encouraging.

To reach the tunnel, we had to bound across the stream, sidestep crevices filled with snoring rock trolls, and steer clear of other trolls who'd fallen asleep out in the open, next to their pickaxes. At one point we passed Jim Dandy's father, Double-knot, curled up against a wheelbarrow. Stump held up a quarter-step, maybe thinking of waking him, but Reliable St. John kept him moving by commenting, "He'd come quietly, I'm sure."

Not far past Double-knot we reached the path leading to our tunnel.

"Not that way," Reliable St. John said.

By then the old lady was balancing herself on the bridge's stone rail, right in front of Bodacious Deepthink's chest, which was rising and lowering in time to her snores. Pulling on the stone glove, the old lady reached for the stone feather in Bo's vest pocket.

No go.

The rock troll's folded hands blocked the way.

To fix that, she sprinkled fairy dust over Bo's hands, both of which began to rise as if leading a sleepwalker. That gave the old lady the opening she needed. Easing the feather out, she held it up for us to see. Stump waved frantically for her to join us, but she wasn't done on the bridge. With her free hand, she grabbed handful after handful of fairy dust and tossed it over the sleeping Bo.

The Great Rock Troll squirmed as though tickled by the fairy dust spattering across her rocky shoulders and hips. The dust melted and glowed as it sank through her tough old hide.

"Let's watch. Let's watch. Let's watch."

Hearing Reliable St. John say that got us moving.

Stump lifted a covered lantern off a nearby wagon and handed it to me. Through a metal loop on its top, I felt the star waking, though at first its glow barely passed through the burlap cover.

By the time I peeked back at the old lady, she had left the bridge and was following us, unwinding white rope from around her waist as she went. About halfway to us, she stopped between two boulders, one of which looked like a giant bunny standing on its ears, the other like an oversize gumball machine. She knotted one end of the rope around the bunny's ears, laid the middle of it across the path, and looped the other end loosely around the gumball machine.

"What's she doing there?" Stump asked.

"It's for tripping," I said.

"Trolls don't fall," Reliable stated.

I was relieved to hear that lie, though the old lady's handiwork did leave me with one question. What good would the rope do while flat on the ground?

That's where the old lady left it, though. Wheeling around, she headed back toward Bodacious Deepthink. Stump tried pssting at her, but with all the snoring trolls around us, it was wasted breath. This time she avoided the bridge, where Bo was still slightly aglow, and bounded over the black stream, headed for the corral. Once there, she swung the wooden gate wide open.

No rhinos rushed to join her.

The bigger rhinos tried bumping and shoving the smaller ones forward, but the ones being pushed dug their hooves in and held back. Farthest from the gate stood Duke, defiantly munching on Farmer Bailey's hay.

All at once the pushing and shoving ceased.

Back on the bridge, Bodacious Deepthink was beginning to swell and rise like a hot-air balloon. Her shoulders and arms were following her hands upward. Lagging behind were her legs and hips. The old lady dashed back to throw handfuls of dust over the rock troll's lower half.

And still the Great Rock Troll slept. As she lifted up, she mumbled and smacked her flinty lips as though sampling something in a lovely dream. The way her body creaked as it expanded and rose, it was a wonder she didn't wake herself.

For every inch she lifted, the rhinos crowded an inch closer to the gate.

At about ten feet above the bridge, Bodacious Deepthink leveled off, bigger than ever. The rhino herd had edged up to the open gate, though not a horn farther. To show them that everything was safe, the old lady trotted right under the floating rock troll.

Still, no one followed, not even Uncle Floyd. Stopping beneath Bodacious, the old lady waved to them like a tourist. By then the fairy dust had sifted all the way through Bo, making her underside glow faintly as sparkling gold and green specks began to flake off her. Ever so slightly, Bodacious Deepthink began to slowly settle back down.

It was Uncle Floyd who summoned his courage first. Butt-ing his way to the front of the herd, he shuffled across the bridge, passing directly beneath Bodacious Deepthink without a scratch. Weak from hunger, he had to pull up several times to catch his breath, and once he even tripped, crashing to his knees. No matter. Bodacious Deepthink snoozed on.

As soon as Uncle Floyd cleared the bridge, Stump whipped the burlap feed sack off the lantern I was holding and knocked the glass with a knuckle. The shooting star inside came to life, shining like a beacon, and the old lady shoved Uncle Floyd down the path toward it. He didn't have any fast in him—barely any slow—but it was a start.

Seeing that, all the bullies but Duke broke for the bridge at once, shoving and pushing and tripping to get across first. A huge rhino jam followed, right beneath Bodacious Deepthink. Thank goodness she was snoring loud as ever and never heard the commotion.

Maybe the rhinos would have sorted everything out sooner or later. Bodacious Deepthink wasn't sinking that fast, and one or two of the rhinos, with some help from the old lady, did spurt free of the herd and gallop after Uncle Floyd. But then Duke looked up from his bale of hay, saw that he was being left behind, and bellowed out with all his might, "Hey! What about me?"

He wasn't satisfied with yelling either. Lowering his horn, he barreled out of the corral to plow into the back of the herd with all his might. The collision caused the middle of the herd to buckle upward, pushing a rhino wearing a baseball cap onto the backs of the others.

By then Bodacious Deepthink had sunk to a height of seven or eight feet above the bridge. The horn of the lifted rhino stabbed her bottom, and that poke did what all the bickering and shouting had failed to. The Great Rock Troll woke.

fifty

BLUE·WINGS

Rubbing her eyes, Bodacious Deepthink tried sitting up. That was a bust. Her middle went down, her two ends up.

"WHAT THE . . ."

Feeling a poke to her underside, she patted beneath herself and found her prize herd of rhinos about to escape. She cut loose with a roar that shook rocks from the cavern's walls.

The rhino with the baseball cap lurched across the backs of the others and jumped for it. A couple of rhinos at the front of the pileup broke free to pound after him. At the back of the herd, Duke kept right on ramming away, which cleared some space too.

All at once, the logjam broke loose and the herd stampeded for freedom, forcing the old lady to jump off the path. Uncle Floyd was nearly trampled.

Bodacious Deepthink twisted, grabbing for them, but the squirming shook up the fairy dust still inside her, making her swell and rise. Plus, she kept filling her lungs to bellow. The extra air made her go up even faster.

"STOP THEM! STOP THEM!! STOP THEM!!!"

Maybe Bodacious Deepthink only screamed it once and the rest were echoes. Either way, all the shouts had trolls staggering out of holes, rubbing sleep from their eyes, and shouting back:

"Who's them?"

"What's them?"

"Where's them?"

Every corner of the cavern had trolls whipping burlap covers off lanterns. With the growing light, there was plenty to see and nowhere to hide.

The two fastest rhinos had already reached the tunnel entrance and were fighting over who would squeeze through the gap first.

"Me!"

"No, me!"

They wouldn't listen to a thing that Stump or I said, not even when Stump broke rocks over their heads. Behind them, the rest of the herd was gaining fast. Duke had used his weight to bull his way to the middle of the pack, but Uncle Floyd was falling behind with every step. Handing the lantern to Stump, I dashed to help my uncle, though reaching him wasn't easy. A herd of stampeding bullies doesn't make room for anyone, and Duke, seeing his chance, head-butted me off the path.

Up above, Bodacious Deepthink rolled from side to side, squirming to see everything. The rocking back and forth shook up the fairy dust inside her even more, sending her all the higher. With a better view, she had more to shout about.

"GET THOSE RHINOS! GET THAT GIRL! THAT OLD LADY! GET HER! AND GET ME DOWN!"

Every rock troll in the place gawked upward, with a mouth like an open rain barrel. Thudding against a ledge, Bo grabbed ahold of it and cracked off chunks to hurl at the trolls below, which sent them screaming after us.

By then I'd reached Uncle Floyd, who'd made it to the rope the old lady had laid across the path.

"You can do it," I said, waving him on.

"Better leave me," he croaked.

"To them?" The trolls were closing in on us.

Rock trolls aren't built for speed any more than a boulder is, but just like a boulder headed downhill, once they start rolling, they stay rolling, gaining speed as they go.

Uncle Floyd took one look and started shuffling again, though first he had to step over the old lady's rope. His hooves had so little oomph in them that I had to help lift his two rear ones over the rope. Once past the rope, he found enough breath to say, "The rope. Stretch it."

Now I understood why the old lady hadn't pulled it tight earlier. The rhinos had to clear it before it would do us any good. Giving Uncle Floyd one last push, I scrambled back to the rope, reaching it barely a dozen steps ahead of the lead rock trolls. They would have had me if the old lady hadn't come to the rescue.

Climbing up on the bridge railing, she whipped out her slingshot and started shooting out lanterns. With each pop and crash of glass, a new shooting star escaped.

"SAVE THE LANTERNS!" Bodacious Deepthink thundered.

That order went against her first orders about stopping the herd and getting me and pulling her down. Trolls skidded to a halt everywhere, confused.

Forgetting about the rope, I yanked out my slingshot and went after the glass lanterns too. My every third or fourth shot nailed a lantern and set a star loose. Freed-up stars whizzed and spun all over the place, sparking off walls and forcing rock trolls to dive for cover. Before long, some began finding their way up the hole leading to Farmer Bailey's pasture. The cave slowly dimmed.

The old lady kept on firing her slingshot, even as rock trolls advanced on her from everywhere. At the last instant, when about to be grabbed, she flung her slingshot at the nearest troll, beaning him on the snout. "Shoo!"

Reaching into a pocket, she tossed a handful of fairy dust over the stream and leaped into it just as three rock trolls jumped for her.

The old lady floated in the fairy dust, soaking all the colors up. From her finger, she pulled off her silver ring, which instantly grew to the size of a crown, and placed it on her head. As soon as the crown touched her white hair, she glowed like sunrise over a snowy field. At the same time, she started to shrink.

Rubbing my eyes didn't change anything.

The smaller she got, the stronger the old lady glowed. In seconds, she was no bigger than my hand, with a pair of blue wings beating on her back.

"A BLUE-WING?" Bodacious Deepthink screamed, outraged. "IN MY HOUSE? GET HER!"

Troll hands grabbed for the old lady, getting air. From lantern to lantern she looped, opening their doors with both hands and standing back as the stars burst out. I laughed to see it, then got busy with my slingshot, helping out as best I could.

"GET THE STONE BIRDS!" Bodacious screamed as the cavern dimmed more.

A small mob of rock trolls began tugging on an iron grate in the cavern floor, waking up something below that screeched worse than busted violins.

When the grate popped up, out burst three dark creatures that were chicken-size and made of stone — gritty stuff with jagged edges. Steering wasn't their strong suit, not with all the stone feathers plucked from their wings, but once airborne, they zoomed after the old lady, zeroing in on her from behind.

"Look out!" I yelled.

All the cheering and jeering of the rock trolls, along with the stone birds screeching, drowned me out. I held my breath, expecting the worst until the old lady dipped at the last instant and the fastest bird went barreling past her.

The chase was on.

Again and again, stone beaks snapped where the old lady had been. Two rock trolls got turned to stone when the birds overshot the old lady and bounced off them instead. One touch from those birds petrified the trolls as solid as my grandpa.

I turned my slingshot on them without luck. One time I connected, but the gravel bounced harmlessly off the bird's back.

Then, with only three lanterns left, the old lady began to tire, causing her glow to flicker. She wobbled before one of the remaining lanterns as the stone birds closed. Her glow winked out. I gasped. The stone birds screeched.

At the last possible second the old lady's glow flashed on and she lifted away. Two of the birds crashed into the lantern with their beaks. The third bird plowed into their stone tail feathers. Shattered glass exploded everywhere, followed by the freed shooting star.

Aside from the lantern Stump held back at the tunnel, only one other lantern was still blazing. An angry knot of rock trolls protected it with pickaxes.

"Shoot it," the old lady called out, whizzing as close to me as she dared without getting caught.

Ducking, I caught a glimpse of her face, which looked centuries younger and as beautiful as someone who's famous for being beautiful. By then I'd emptied my sack of gravel and had to hunt for stones on the cavern floor, but a large troll protected their last lantern with a shovel, knocking down my every shot.

The old lady's glow began flickering again, leaving her no time or strength to offer more advice. The stone birds were closing fast.

When she rose up the hole to Farmer Bailey's pasture, the stone birds screeched right after her, pecking at her tiny heels.

The cave fell silent like an old church. That didn't last long.

"GET ME DOWN!" bellowed Bodacious Deepthink.

fifty one

TASTY

Not a one of the rhinos stranded outside the tunnel knew what taking turns meant. They all tried to cram through the tunnel mouth at once, no matter how loud or often Stump shouted, "Back off!" Duke thrashed about in the thick of the frenzy, kicking up the biggest fuss of all, and even Uncle Floyd, weak as he was, panicked and tried butting his way ahead.

Every once in a while, Stump gave up shouting and set the lantern aside to yank a rhino back by the tail. If he picked the right tail, his efforts made a slight opening that allowed a different rhino to squirt through the gap and gallop off into the darkness. After twenty or thirty steps, the escaping rhinos either slammed into a wall or another rhino, unable to see either. The ones left behind wailed all the louder, even though within minutes the freed rhinos came limping back to demand the lantern.

"We can't see a thing!" the bruised rhinos clamored. "Hand over the lantern."

"No way!" Duke screamed back.

At which point every rhino on the outside went back to pushing and shoving and squealing and checking over their shoulders with bugged eyes. Stump was the only one who showed any sense at all, which left me feeling unexplainably proud. (No time to wonder about that, though.)

Bodacious Deepthink kept right on barking orders from on high. She had her rock trolls tie together a long rope made of hay-bale twine, bootlaces, and leather reins, then had her bat earrings fly one end up to her so that rock trolls could pull her down. They didn't reel her in anywhere near fast enough to suit the Great Rock Troll, but they made progress.

Slow as Stump was squeezing rhinos into the tunnel, we needed more time. I tried buying it by tying the old lady's rope tautly across the path, but I couldn't get a knot to stick. The rope was slippery and felt as if it might have been soaped or — more likely — was under some kind of spell. It kept drooping toward the cavern floor, hanging so loose and low that it wouldn't have tripped a shadow.

And then time ran out.

Bodacious Deepthink landed on the cavern floor with a thud followed by a bounce. Her pockets had to be stuffed with small boulders to keep her from floating off again.

"AFTER THEM!" Bodacious Deepthink howled, charging ahead.

Still full of fairy dust, she bounced as though on a trampoline. The other rock trolls did their best to drag themselves after her.

"PUDDING!" Bo yelled. "PUDDING!"

"And cream!" her trolls answered. "And cream!"

The pounding of Bo's feet, along with all the shouting about pudding and cream, soon drowned out even the bickering of the rhinos.

And still I couldn't get a knot to stick. In the end, I had no choice but to hold the rope tight myself, pulling back with all my might. Bodacious Deepthink was soon upon me, too focused on her escaping rhinos to notice me or the rope I was stretching across the path.

Her lead foot, looking as big as most people's front steps, sailed past me, clearing the rope by inches. For a heart-flipping second I thought her back foot would do likewise, but at the last instant the rope stretched up — I swear — and snagged her little toe, tripping her.

Her weight fell so hard against the rope that she ripped it out of my hands, flipping me backwards.

She teetered, fighting for balance, and might have regained it if Jim Dandy's father hadn't stepped out of the shadows, grabbed the loose end of the rope, and dragged it around Bo twice, lashing her ankles together tightly.

Tim-ber!

First she fell slowly, then all at once, like a tower of teacups given a shove. All the way down she made a horrible, strangled cry:

"I-

E-

E-

E-

E-

E-

E-

E-

E-

E-

E-

E!"

Hard as she hit the ground, I thought she might shatter, but she only lost some chips off her elbows and knees, which smacked first.

There was a windy "ga-rumph-umph" at the end, but the grunt didn't belong to Bodacious Deepthink. It came from Double-knot

Eel-tongue, who'd gotten tangled up with the rope himself and trapped beneath the falling troll. The way the Great Rock Troll landed, she must have broken most everything inside him that was breakable and popped everything else.

"WHO??!" Bo screamed.

The answer to that lay trapped beneath her, trying to tell me something. Leaning forward, I heard Double-knot wheeze, "Jim Dandy . . . run."

I heard him say no more, for by then Bodacious Deepthink had found me. First her eyes, all gold and cold, found me, and then her hands, all hard and rock, found me.

"YOU!" Bo bellowed.

Brushing Double-knot aside, she grabbed me by the waist and, struggling to her feet, lifted me up to her face. Her breath ground into my cheeks and burned the tip of my nose.

"Tasty," she hooted, giving me a shake.

"Share her!" the other rock trolls begged.

Not knowing what else to do, I blurted, "I know a riddle."

fifty two

THE RIDDLE

All the rock trolls around me started grinning strangely and whispering over their shoulders, and rubbing their tummies. None of which I cared to think about at all.

"A riddle?" Bodacious Deepthink sneered. "Who told you to try that?"

"I forget."

"Oh, I think not," Bo corrected. "Little blue-wing fairies, I'd say. Do you know what happens if I answer this riddle of yours?"

"Something terrible?" I guessed, trying not to cringe.

"That's right," Bo said with a rock-splitting laugh. "But not terrible for me."

"And what if you *can't* answer it?" I asked.

That brought a smirk to Bodacious Deepthink's wide mouth and made the trolls behind her hoot with glee.

"That's never happened," Bo said smugly.

The surrounding trolls seconded that, sounding proud of how nasty and smart and cunning their leader was.

"But what if you can't?" I insisted, squirming against her hands.

"Why, then," Bo said as she squeezed me tighter, "you'll be free to go, of course."

"And the rhinos? They can go with me?"

"Why, of course," she answered, her voice cold. "And the riddle?"

Pressing my eyes shut, I strained to recall what Jim Dandy's mother had told me. At first I drew a blank that had the trolls slapping their knees and roaring with laughter as my lips moved but nothing came out.

"Ah," Bo mocked, "the famous riddle without words. The answer to that is . . ."

The trolls gleefully sang, "Pudding, pudding, pudding," which did wonders for my memory. The riddle popped right out of me:

> What dreams of red,
> Mines gold in veins,
> Makes a good stew,
> And always complains?

What followed was silence, if you blocked out the rhinos bickering in the background.

Every troll cocked his or her head and leaned forward as if able to hear what Bodacious Deepthink was thinking. The Great Rock Troll herself lifted her chin toward the ceiling and closed her eyes in concentration.

When Bodacious Deepthink started tapping her foot, the nearest trolls straightened in alarm, reporting the holdup over their shoulders in whispers. The Great Rock Troll's head whipped toward the whisperers so fast that they crammed their own fists in their mouths to shut themselves up.

"Some of the fools in back must not have heard your pitiful little riddle," Bodacious Deepthink croaked. "Would you mind repeating it for them?"

I repeated it, noticing as I did that the Great Rock Troll was mouthing the words with me.

"Louder," she said.

I turned up my volume, understanding now that she was stalling.

"Tricky little thing, aren't you?" Bodacious clenched her teeth.

"Take as long as you need," I offered generously. The longer she fussed, the more rhinos Stump got into the tunnel.

"I don't need time!" Bo stamped her foot.

But she did need it, and the longer she ground on the answer, the more restless the other rock trolls grew. The nearest ones began edging backwards. The farthest ones slipped behind boulders, perhaps knowing something I didn't. And all the while Bodacious Deepthink was squeezing me until I felt like a tube of toothpaste about to blow. Then, without warning, she gave me a shake and cried, "I've got it. Worms!"

"Wrong."

"LIAR!" she screamed.

"Afraid not," I said, fighting for breath.

"Then you're a cheater. The answer must be my cook, but he's never made a good stew. He can barely burn porridge."

"Wrong again," I gasped.

Hearing that threw Bo into a blind rage. Groaning, she slapped both hands over her eyes as if she couldn't bear to look at me, or the world. Of course, to do that she had to let go of me. Without waiting for her next guess, I sucked down a breath and stumbled off.

By then the number of rhinos still outside the tunnel had dwindled to three. Behind me, Bo stomped her foot down so hard that the entire cavern quaked, shaking one more rhino through the tunnel mouth. That left my cousin Duke and Uncle Floyd trapped outside. I was almost to them when I heard the loudest shout yet from behind me.

"WAIT!!!!"

Turning, I saw that Bo had uncovered her eyes and was staring down at Double-knot's lifeless body.

"RIVER TROLLS!!!!" she shouted, as if that explained everything.

"Yes? Yes?" the mob of trolls answered, peeking out from behind boulders.

"THINK," Bo shouted, slapping the side of her head as if trying to put out a fire raging between her ears. "THINK!"

I didn't bother with thinking but stuck with running, yelling as I went, "Hurry, hurry."

For once my cousin Duke took my advice. Kicking Uncle Floyd aside, he launched himself straight into the gap. At the same time that he hit the mouth of the tunnel, Bodacious Deepthink roared, "LEECHES! IT'S LEECHES!"

A victory cheer rose from the trolls just as Duke found out another reason that he shouldn't have been stuffing himself full of hay. Plump and round as he was, he plugged the mouth of the tunnel all by himself.

"GRAB THEM!" Bo screamed.

Trolls came whooping after us, with Bodacious Deepthink leading the charge. A row of fire trucks couldn't have put out the blaze in her eyes.

From inside the tunnel, the rhino herd shouted for the lantern. Stump stunned everyone by leaning his shoulder into my cousin's rump and pushing as hard as he could.

"Pull him through," Stump ordered the other rhinos.

That hardly worked either. Hooves aren't much help when it comes to grabbing and pulling. I arrived, throwing my shoulder next to Stump's, but Duke stayed wedged tight.

It was Reliable St. John who saved the day by calling out from Stump's shoulder, "I wouldn't lift him."

That's when we noticed that the tunnel mouth was widest in the middle, narrowest at the top and bottom. Backing Duke out took some sweat, but we managed despite Duke's threats. Then Stump crouched down on his hands and knees, filling the bottom of the gap so that Duke could step on his back. As he crouched, Stump grumbled that his brother Duckwad had made him bend over the exact same way so that he could reach the slug jar.

The only good thing about all this? I didn't have time to dwell on how I'd once talked my younger sister Tessa into the same maneuver to reach the cookie jar.

"Just do it," Duke thundered, as Bodacious Deepthink huffed nearer and nearer.

So Stump did it, allowing Duke to step on his back and crash through the gap. My cousin blundered off into the darkness without so much as a thank-you.

By then Bodacious Deepthink was screaming, "INTO THE POT! INTO THE POT! INTO THE POT!" As a rallying cry, it worked wonders. Trolls were pouring forward from everywhere, crying for justice and pudding.

Grabbing the lantern, I leaped over Stump and into the tunnel, waving for Uncle Floyd to follow.

"Now you!" I called.

He charged toward us as fast as his wobbly old legs could manage, but as he tried hopping onto Stump's back, one of his ankles buckled. He hit the gap low and way off-center.

There followed a smoosh and a *whoomph*. I jumped back. Stump got rammed into the tunnel, with Uncle Floyd's shapeless hat flying after him. The rock stalagmites and stalactites stayed put, and so did Uncle Floyd, wedged crossways.

Oh, how Bodacious Deepthink roared with joy to see the fix we were in.

"MY LITTLE DUMPLING!"

"Squirm!" I ordered, grabbing ahold of Uncle Floyd's horn and pulling with all my might.

"Breathe in!" Stump shouted.

But it was no good. Uncle Floyd might as well have been Super-Glued in place.

"Leave me," Uncle Floyd said. "Go."

He didn't come anywhere near shouting it. In fact, he said it so low that I could barely hear him above all the rock trolls stomping closer. But I guess the important thing was that he meant it. He wanted me and all the others to get away no matter what. He even sounded a little proud that we would get away because of him.

It qualified as a genuine, unselfish act of kindness.

The pop and flash that followed were loud and bright as a rocket blasting off for Pluto. There was plenty of white smoke too, which smelled like peaches and cream.

When the smoke cleared, Uncle Floyd stood before us, holding his hands up as if he'd never seen such amazing things before. Which he hadn't. Or at least not for way more than a hundred years, he hadn't. You see, those hands had fingers, not hooves. He'd turned back into a young man, one dressed in a badly ripped pair of black pants that were held up — sort of — with a twine belt.

"It's me!" he cried.

"It is!" I cried.

"STOP!" cried you-know-who.

fifty three

FASTER. FASTER. FASTER

There we were, packed in a black tunnel—with a herd of bullies, one lantern, and a cave cricket who couldn't help lying.

Grabbing the lantern, Stump passed to the front of the line as Reliable St. John urged him, "Go slower. Go slower."

The rhinos lined up behind Stump, whining and griping all the while. Each one of them was convinced that he or she should be carrying the lantern. When Uncle Floyd and I tried following Stump up front, several rhinos blocked our way, snapping, "End of the line!"

Uncle Floyd didn't mind, though. He was too tickled with the return of his fingers and toes to care. At one point, he said to me, "Wait till Huntington hears about this." I didn't exactly get around to explaining that his brother, my Great-Great-Great-Grandfather Huntington Bridgewater, had been dead and buried for around a hundred years. Not too far behind us, Bodacious Deepthink was bellowing at her trolls.

"'FRAIDY CATS! CRYBABIES!"

The rock trolls weren't too eager to pop through a black hole where a herd of escaping rhinoceroses had just disappeared.

After we rounded a couple of bends, the rock trolls' shouts faded to a rumble. By then the tunnel, stretching out in darkness before and behind us, already seemed too long to me. Cut out of limestone, the walls sparkled as the lantern passed, but way back at the end of the line, where Uncle Floyd and I bumped along, the sparkles had already faded to a dull yellow-green, the color of split-pea soup. The tunnel was damp and smelly as soup too, last year's batch. Its ceiling rose higher than I could jump. Its sides stretched far enough apart for two rhinos to walk side by side, if they didn't squabble. Fat chance.

At least we couldn't hear any footsteps echoing in the inkiness behind us, though we didn't get to feel safe for long. An explosion suddenly knocked us down, followed by a dusty wind that blew over us. When the blast's echoes quit filling our ears and the wind died off, the ringing of pickaxes breaking rock could be heard.

They must have been widening the mouth of the tunnel to accommodate Bodacious Deepthink's swollen body, for the Great Rock Troll was screeching something over and over. Straining, I could make out just one word.

"FASTER! FASTER! FASTER!"

Only Reliable St. John, now riding atop the lantern, had something to say to that — "I think we should wait for her."

Taking the hint, Stump started trotting. The rest of us bumbled along behind.

When we reached the first fork in the tunnel, we all held up while Stump asked Reliable St. John which way to go.

"To the right," the cave cricket said.

Stump swung the lantern toward the right fork, which was the smaller of the two.

"You sure?" Stump asked.

"No," Reliable St. John answered.

Satisfied, Stump led us down the left fork, though there was plenty of second-guessing in the line behind him.

From then on, every time we reached a fork in the tunnel, Stump asked the same questions and Reliable St. John lied the same answers. In general, the tunnels headed up and the air grew ever so faintly fresher, though every once in a while we hit a stretch that dipped downward and the air turned fouler. Twice we passed small side tunnels down which we could hear stone birds singing far away. At those times everybody moved faster, especially Duke, who had shoved his way up front and who claimed over and over that he could hear the rock trolls getting closer. Maybe he could.

Bodacious Deepthink and her trolls had to have known some shortcuts. At times I thought I could hear voices or footsteps through the walls myself. But maybe not. Underground, in total darkness, sound comes from everywhere and nowhere all at once.

Eventually we reached a three-way fork in the tunnel and came to a total stop, for the extra tunnel meant it took longer to sort through Reliable St. John's lies. When the cricket said we should take the tunnel on the right, there were still two tunnels on the left to choose from.

"Should we take this one?" Stump pointed at the nearest of the two remaining tunnels.

"By all means," Reliable St. John said, "if you want to get lost."

"That must mean it's the way to go," Stump reckoned. "Since we don't want to get lost."

But before we could get started, a toe-curling squeal erupted from the herd. Rock trolls had sprung out of the tunnel on the right and were dragging the closest rhino away.

"I'm too skinny!" the rhino cried, kicking and crashing about. "Way too skinny!"

"Save him!" Uncle Floyd shouted.

And that was when the first of twenty-eight more amazing things happened in that tunnel. One of the rhinos in the middle of the herd lowered his horn and charged to the rescue.

"Fool," Duke said.

Just then the rhino reached the trolls and there was a bang and a flash as loud and bright as another rocket blasting off for Pluto. There was smoke too, along with the sweet smell of peaches and cream. The trolls dropped the rhino they'd snatched and fled for their lives.

What caused the explosion?

A second act of genuine kindness.

After the echoes faded and the smoke cleared, a short, chunky kid in a tattered Little League uniform stood where the charging rhino had been. He was grinning wildly while rubbing a thumb across his forehead. His horn had vanished—not even a knob marked the spot.

fifty four

RELIABLE ST. JOHN'S SONG

From then on there was no shortage of genuine acts of kindness in that tunnel as the remaining rhinos charged at rock trolls who sprang out from side tunnels.

A few bullies acted more interested in being changed back into a boy or girl than in sacrificing themselves to save someone else. When they rushed forward, they stayed rhinos, and the trolls gleefully dragged them off, hooting and laughing above the wailing. But another rhino always unselfishly stepped forward to save the day with a *true* act of genuine kindness. Eventually, even the selfish bullies learned their lesson, and the next time they tried a rescue, their motives were purer. Smoke and the sweet smell of peaches and cream rolled off them.

By the time we reached the end of the tunnel, there was only one rhino left, along with twenty-eight kids—twenty-nine if you counted me. The remaining rhino wasn't shy about sharing his opinion, but then he never had been.

"Don't expect me to protect you," Duke blustered. "I plan on staying just the way I am."

"You might want to think twice about that," Stump told him.

"Jim Dandy's nowhere near the friend you've been pretending he is, even when he's not stone."

Duke didn't care for that idea, but he didn't bother arguing about it either. He was too busy snorting at the dead-end wall that Reliable St. John had run us into.

Worse yet, we could see a lantern drawing closer from behind us. Shouts could be heard. Bodacious Deepthink kind of shouts.

"Faster. Faster! FASTER!"

"What should we do?" Stump asked Reliable St. John.

"Go back," the cave cricket advised.

"Impossible!" everyone cried, forgetting it was a cave cricket talking.

Right away Stump asked the cricket how we were supposed to walk through a wall.

"Not with a song," Reliable St. John answered.

"I think we could all use a song right about now," Stump told the cricket. "If you don't mind."

But before Reliable St. John could even clear his tiny throat, Bodacious Deepthink and her trolls roared around the last corner behind us.

"MY RHINOS?" Bo screeched.

We all crowded behind what was left of her rhinos, namely Duke. He, in turn, tried backing through us.

"WHERE ARE THEY?"

In the silence that followed, a single small voice answered.

> Jewel box, jewel box
>   of the earth
> Open up and send
>   us forth.

Reliable St. John was singing the rock wall open.

The cricket didn't have much of a singing voice, but apparently he didn't need one. The wall at our backs began to slide upward like a garage door.

"GET THAT CRICKET!" Bodacious Deepthink yelled.

But having had enough of smoke and peaches, not a single rock troll took so much as a baby step forward. Bo lifted a couple of nearby trolls up, hurling them at us, but as soon as they regained their feet, they scrambled for cover.

Outraged, Bodacious Deepthink took a deep breath and began singing. The nightingales had fled her voice, leaving something foul and creaky in their place.

> Jewel box, jewel box
> > of the earth
> Close your lid
> > or feel a curse.

The stone wall started soundlessly lowering.

Up and down the wall went, as first Reliable St. John, then Bodacious Deepthink, sang. At its highest point, the wall never raised more than a foot, which was hardly enough to crawl under, but was more than enough to tease us with whiffs of fresh air and glimpses of sunlight and snatches of birdsong.

Reliable St. John finally stopped singing long enough to call out, "I wouldn't plug her mouth."

"What wouldn't you plug it with?" Stump asked.

"A rock."

"I wouldn't either," Stump agreed, but at the same time he picked up a good-size rock, almost a boulder and, staggering forward, tossed it with all his might.

The rock hung in the air for nearly forever before landing in Bo's mouth just as she was cutting loose with "feel a curse." There it stayed, wedged tight, but although the rock put a stop to Bo's singing, it didn't keep her from grabbing. With one swipe of her hand, she had Stump by his ankle, holding him upside down as if looking for a saucepot to dunk him in.

"Do something," I cried to Duke.

What happened next was the second biggest surprise of my life. A glazed look overtook Duke's eyes, and then he actually did something, though first he had to grouse about it.

"Little fool," he muttered, though he seemed to talking to Stump, not me.

But then he sucked down a deep breath, lowered his head, and charged.

That was Duke, my cousin . . . charging a rock troll.

Bodacious Deepthink knew just what to do. Turning surprisingly light-footed, she sidestepped Duke's charge, snatched up one of his hind legs with her free hand, and swept him into the air. So now Duke dangled from one of her hands, Stump from the other, and her mood was merry as could be. Puffing out her cheeks, she spit the small boulder out of her mouth and got ready to crow.

She wasn't quick enough.

Before she got out one peep there came a flash and a bang and as much smoke as one last rocket blasting off for Pluto would have made. No sweet smell of peaches and cream accompanied it, though. What rolled over us this time was a rotting smell of river muck and fish scales. When the smoke cleared, I found out why and nearly fainted. The biggest surprise of my life had arrived.

You see, Duke wasn't a rhino anymore.

He wasn't exactly my cousin, either.

His act of genuine kindness had turned him into a river troll.

fifty-five

THE RETURN OF DUCKWAD FISHFLY

Duckwad?" Stump yelled, stunned.

"This is all your fault," complained the river troll hanging upside down in Bodacious Deepthink's other hand. One genuine act of kindness appeared to be Duke's limit, whether he was human or river troll.

"QUIET!" Bodacious Deepthink roared, shaking the two river trolls hard enough to cross their eyes. Holding the new river troll up to her snout, she demanded, "WHERE'D YOU COME FROM?"

"Over there?" Duke said, pointing a shaky claw toward us.

"I think maybe he's my brother," Stump meekly suggested.

Even with the two river trolls dangling upside down, you couldn't help but see a strong family resemblance around their knotty brows and foamy snouts.

"WHAT?"

"Your curse turned him human years ago," Stump said. "When he got his months mixed up. But now, having stood up to you, he's back."

"WE'LL SEE ABOUT THAT!" Bodacious Deepthink bellowed, and she started swinging Duckwad around and around, as if about to break him open against a wall.

Strangely enough, hearing all this filled me with such a surge of hope that I nearly burst. For one thing, it meant I could quit worrying about being Duckwad. Much as I'd come to like Stump, I didn't really want to be his brother. I was kind of used to being who I was, even if I was totally different from my sisters, even if turtles and toads and snakes were always looking me up. Finding out that Duke was Duckwad thrilled me so much that I did a foolish thing. I took a step forward and screamed at the top of my lungs, "Save them!"

"HUH?" Bodacious Deepthink said, looking up.

All the other kids stepped forward with me, shouting things like:

"We will!"

"Let's show her!"

"Pudding, my foot!"

And while all that shouting was going on, Reliable St. John kept right on singing the rock wall up. Not a one of us turned and bolted for daylight, though we could have. High as the door had climbed, we wouldn't even have had to duck on the way out. Late-afternoon sunlight was streaming in from outside, making us feel as big as our shadows, which were like giants.

We started for Bodacious Deepthink as one, stepping slowly but gaining speed.

We stomped our feet.

We pounded our chests.

We howled like the wildest hyenas alive.

We sounded so awful that Bodacious Deepthink dropped Stump and Duckwad to cover her ears. The two river trolls rolled to safety, but we didn't. We stormed on toward danger, determined to teach Bodacious Deepthink, the Great Rock Troll, that she'd better think at least twice before trying to fatten up kids of any kind ever again.

I'll never be sure if it was us or the sun pouring over our shoulders that frightened Bodacious Deepthink so terribly. But the Great

Rock Troll spun around with a yelp and stumbled away, climbing over the backs of other rock trolls to clatter off into the darkness. Her trolls followed but not before I grabbed up a small rock, whipped out my slingshot, and smashed their last lantern with one pure-luck shot.

Turning toward our lantern, I broke it open too.

The two shooting stars did several figure eights of joy before whizzing over our heads and out of the cave. We were watching them go when Reliable St. John called out, "I'm sure the door will stay open forever."

In one mad dash we raced out of the cave and into the great outdoors, which on that day seemed far greater and fresher and grander than ever before. While we'd been underground, the first green day of spring had sprung. Leaves had popped out everywhere. All around me stood kids in tattered, ripped clothes, who were laughing as if green were the funniest color in the world.

Way below us, at the bottom of the valley, the Mississippi flashed in the sunlight. From a distance, it looked blue, not brown, and pretty as a flower. We headed that way, calling hello to the birds and trees and anything else that cared to listen. We sniffed deep on every breeze that came our way. Everything we heard made us laugh. We headed down there arm in arm and wearing one grin that was twenty-nine people, two river trolls, and one cricket wide.

fifty six

ONE HUNDRED & FIFTY·FIVE YEARS

Back at the highway the old lady and her brother were waiting in the van. The silver ring was back on her left hand, and her right hand wore a stone glove that held a rock feather. When I asked about the rock birds, she pointed at the ground and said, "Back where they belong."

The old man offered us all a ride home, and how we all fit in the back of that van, I can't say. The answer to that goes beyond geometry. There was even room for Stump to lie down on the floor so that he wouldn't scare people in passing cars. Duckwad could have joined him. There was room. But he said he'd had enough sunlight for that year and crossed the highway to wade into the river without even waving goodbye. The river took him back without a ripple of complaint, which goes to show just how big a river it is.

Two kids hopped off in Big Rock, and the rest of us hung on till Blue Wing, where the old man had to pull over every few blocks to drop someone off. Excited shouts of "I'm home!" filled the air behind us.

A handful of kids couldn't find their families. Too much time had gone by and their parents had moved away or passed on. We delivered them to Sheriff Tommy Pope, who told them not to worry.

The sheriff's department kept a missing-person file on every one of them, and the files listed where their families had moved to or the location of their nearest living relative.

By the time we got to Duke's house, the whole town was abuzz. We trooped through the open back door, the old lady leading the way with the stone feather. She had Grandpa B back to breathing in a jiffy. Tipping his hat to us, he stretched and said he'd never felt more rested. Aunt Phyllis and Uncle Norm took the news about Duke way better than I'd expected. They didn't even mind that he couldn't be bothered to come say goodbye. Actually, they looked kind of relieved.

Jim Dandy claimed that he'd always known there was something familiar about Duke. All three crickets called out, "No, there wasn't!" Biz took off in a lather the instant he heard of Duckwad's return, crying out, "He's got a head start on finding our fathers." Stump and Jim Dandy streaked after him, though Stump did pause long enough at the back door to say, "Thanks."

Such thoughtfulness is rare, and I knew I was going to miss him.

The deputy and Dr. E. O. Moneybaker followed the trolls, in hot pursuit but losing sight of them before they'd even cleared the backyard fence. Men of science and the law just didn't have eyes for anything rivery. Whether women of science and the law had any sharper vision, I can't say. But I can testify that despite failing eyesight, Grandpa B saw Biz, Jim Dandy, and Stump's escape just fine, even cheered them on. Dr. Moneybaker stormed back to the house and phoned One-shot, ordering up a fresh batch of photographs. One-shot's answer made the doctor gripe, "I knew that!"

Old Duff couldn't stop wagging his tail, and the sparrow perched atop Uncle Norm's head lit out the back door as fast as wings could carry him. The old lady and her brother cleared out pretty quick too, claiming they were needed elsewhere, but before they drove off, the old lady placed her hands on my shoulders for one last peek into my eyes. When I checked out her eyes, all I saw was the river, peaceful and lovely as a daydream.

"Crickets?" I asked, wondering what she was seeing. A mysterious smile had curled the corners of her mouth.

"Among other things."

And, patting my cheek, she was gone before I could quiz her further.

Then Grandpa was pulling me home by the arm. When we got back to my house, Mom and Dad pretty near hugged us to pieces before grounding me forever. Even my sisters seemed glad to see me. Mom had been making them feed flies to Three, down in the basement. When I asked if they'd heard anything from Lottie, they rolled their eyes and reminded me that turtles couldn't talk.

Nobody knew what to make of Uncle Floyd. He kept gawking at everything, and bumping into what he wasn't gawking at, and with a goofy grin asking what year it was. According to Grandpa, Uncle Floyd had been gone one hundred and fifty-five years, though he barely looked a day beyond sixteen.

We dressed him up in some of Dad's clothes and set up a cot for him in the basement. When Grandpa lobbied for Uncle Floyd to bunk at his house, Mom exercised veto power, saying that if he was ever going to adjust, he needed to be around people his own age.

"He'd have to set up house in the cemetery for that," Grandpa said.

"You know what I mean," Mom firmly answered. "He looks the same age as Fran and Lillie."

"How you going to pass him off?" Grandpa asked, hanging tough.

"We'll say he's a cousin visiting from Kalamazoo," Mom said, chock-full of surprising answers.

So we had a new member of our family, one who kept us on our toes. He couldn't quit trying to talk to people on TV, or jumping up every time the phone rang, or leaning out a window whenever a jet rumbled by overhead. There were some pluses, though. For one thing, my sisters spent so much time being embarrassed about having a new man around the house that they couldn't be bothered with worrying about me and Three.

—fifty·seven—
THE MISSING FATHERS

All in all, I was pretty well satisfied with events. Maybe that explains what I did several nights later when I heard a *scritch-scritch-scritch* at my bedroom window. Checking, I found Stump clinging to the catalpa tree, looking terrified of heights. I laughed to see him, then sobered when I noticed Biz and Jim Dandy standing below. Duckwad was nowhere in sight.

"We've a favor to ask," Stump said, sheepish about it.

"How big?"

"Not so. We need you to look inside a cabin for us. Shouldn't be too dangerous."

"What's in the cabin?" I asked.

"Maybe our fathers."

"All of them?"

"Could be. You know what it's like trying to figure out what a cricket's saying."

"Not hard, not hard, not hard," sang the crickets on their shoulders.

I crawled out the window before our talking woke someone who might remind me that I was grounded forever. I didn't even ask why they couldn't look in the cabin themselves. That question got answered about two hours later, when we beached our dugout canoes on a sandbar far above Big Rock.

There was a cabin, but between it and us was a ripple in the river that the trolls didn't want any part of. I wasn't too thrilled with it myself. Midnight had come and gone by then, and a quarter-moon gave off enough light to make the ripple wink at us. It wasn't the kind of wink that left anyone feeling comfortable.

"What's that ripple?" I asked.

"It's nothing to worry about," Jim Dandy promised, silky as ever.

"The blue-wing's spell stops there," Stump whispered at my side. "We daren't go beyond it, but it shouldn't be any problem for you."

"Take this," Biz squeaked, holding out an old flashlight.

The flashlight was identical to the old man's flashlight, all the way down to the Day-Glo atomic sticker on its end, but I didn't ask where they'd gotten it. Turning on its beam, which was as bright as a car's headlights, I advanced along the shore with three trolls in tow.

Stopping short of the ripple, I could hear the river rushing over something, but when I shined my light on the water, all I saw was sandy bottom. The line made by the ripple stretched out of sight across the river. At my feet, where the line met the shore, it turned into a mound of sand about the size of what a mole might push up. It cut straight across the island, headed toward the bluffs.

Fifty yards beyond the ripple sagged a tumbledown log cabin that looked as though it'd seen a hundred floods come and go.

"Why would your fathers go there?" I asked.

The three river trolls shook their heads in total bewilderment.

"Emeralds," Reliable St. John answered for them.

"Diamonds," Biz's cricket sang.

"Gold doubloons," added Jim Dandy's cricket.

All lies, of course, but to find out otherwise, I'd have to hike over there in person.

I did feel a tiny tingle as I stepped over the ripple, but other than that, I could have been stepping over a sidewalk crack. The river and valley and sky on the other side looked exactly the same, as did the trolls standing behind me. Jogging, I soon reached the cabin and shined my light through a glassless side window. Inside was nothing but one small room with rotted-out floorboards and junk deposited by the last flood that passed through—pop cans, paper plates, plastic spoons. There was no sign of missing troll fathers or of anything that might have lured them.

Turning around, I was about to call out that there was nothing there when I saw it.

A hole was opening at the base of a huge old cottonwood tree twenty steps behind Stump, Biz, and Jim Dandy.

A rock troll was rumbling out of the hole.

He held a pitchfork. He wore a bib. He looked as though Bodacious Deepthink might be his cute little sister.

I didn't need to shout "Look out!" The only thing quiet about a rock troll that humongous was his manners.

"PUDDING!" he slobbered. "PUDDING!"

"We're not sorry. We're not sorry," sobbed the lucky cave crickets.

Backed up against the ripple, Stump, Biz, and Jim Dandy had nowhere to go but the river. They might have made it too, except that Jim Dandy fainted—this time for real—and Biz thought he was stone again. Something told me they weren't the first river trolls to freeze on that exact same spot. It appeared the crickets' lies had led us into a trap.

True blue to the end, Stump struggled to drag his friends into the river, but there wasn't time. The rock troll was closing fast.

With a whoop, I came running.

That slowed the rock troll for maybe a split second, to laugh. I was about to hurl the flashlight at him, but before I let go, the light beam raked across his face, blinding him. Raising a hand to shield his eyes, he tripped.

"Get down!" I yelled.

Stump shoved Biz on top of Jim Dandy, then dove to sand himself.

The rock troll sailed over them, shooting past the ripple. The bloodcurdling scream he let out at that instant made my ears flap.

"COLD!"

As he tumbled and twisted on the far side of the ripple, his feet splashed into the river and a block of ice instantly formed around them. His wails and writhing went on until he burst into a crackling flame, which according to the old lady was the only way he could keep warm. As he lifted off the ground, his flames grew brighter. In less than a minute he was blinding as a shooting star. Then he began to shrink until, in no time at all, he was small as a shooting star. Pointing skyward, he zoomed out of sight.

Not a one of us blinked or twitched a tail. We were all leaning so far back that we almost toppled over. At last Stump said in a hushed voice, "Is that what happened to our fathers?"

Lost in our own thoughts, each of us gazed upward as if seeing the night sky for the first time.

"That or pudding," Biz squeaked, breaking our trance.

"Hey!" Jim Dandy said, coming to life. "That means we did it. We found 'em."

And then they danced. And sang. I joined in too.

We didn't sound any better than the last time, but at least we weren't at it long. When we started line dancing down the beach, we tripped over the same thing that had sent the rock troll sprawling. We ended up in a giggly pile on the sand, several feet shy of the ripple. At the center of the pile was a large box turtle who had parked right in everyone's way. It was my friend Lottie, come to say hello.

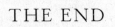

THE END

AFTERWORD

The town of Blue Wing, Minnesota, lies a hundred and twenty some miles downriver from the twin cities of Minneapolis and St. Paul. Mapmakers usually overlook it, but these directions may help: Follow Highway 61 south from St. Paul. Don't be confused by the city of Red Wing — that's a completely different town, with completely different stories. Once past Reads Landing, start paying attention. If you reach the Reno Bottoms without spotting Blue Wing, you've gone too far and will have to backtrack.